Roses On My Doorstep

by

Coreen Picconatto

All Rights Reserved
Copyright ©2003
ISBN 1-59405-030-9
Reproduction in any medium without consent
of the author is expressly prohibited.
Publishing by N2Print
Published and Printed in the United States of America

I would like to dedicate this

to all my friends and family members,

for every one

has been a blessing in my life.

Introduction

This book contains some twists and turns in it. It is a story about a girl named Jane who is in an insane asylum. Jane ends up going back and forth throughout the entire book, both writing about her past and telling you about the present.

In this story Jane ended up falling in love with her best friend's husband in Rome, Italy. All her life what she truly wanted so very much was to be loved. Jane and Larry try to figure out how to tell Lynn that they were in love without hurting her, which seemed impossible.

Jane wrote everything down as she remembered it, only to discover in the end that nothing was as it appeared.

What we are given each day is before us, whether shameful or hurtful. What we decide to do each day is before us. We decide our future, in how we feel or react, and in every situation involving society.

You have to go for your dream—no matter what is in your way!

Roses

On My Doorstep

Chapter One

Hello, I just wanted to start by saying that my name is Jane. Right now I am sitting by a barred window in a locked room. At night they usually do that, just to have us secure. It's a home for the mentally disturbed, slash insane asylum.

Right now I am staring at a tree called the weeping willow and thinking that this is the most beautiful tree that I have ever seen, and thinking how the lines of the tree are so unique, and watching the way it sways in the wind. It's as if it's waving at me, telling me things that no one else knows, like the clouds are green, the sky is brown and the grass is blue.

I have been writing a poem —

Someone

To know you, is to be one
To understand you, is to be everyone

To love you, is like a leaf, something immaterial
The configuration of the design, so primitive
The lines so eccentric

Being that is special
To look at you
And not to think classificational
But to think of you as original!!!

I have been here for two years now and am finally off my medication. Well, at least they still think I take it. I did take it to begin with, but it made me crazy. So I just don't take it any more. The people that work here are actually very nice to me. Especially this guy named Jack; he's 6'3" with black hair, green eyes and built so fine it could make ice melt.

When I first got here, everyone thought I was crazy, insane. But I knew I was fine and was thinking straight. I always have been and I always will be. I guess I will use the time in here to better myself even more.

When I look out of this window, more and more I know the world out there is false—that we're not really here. Who's to say that everything is real out there? We just do so because that is what we were brought up to believe that the sky is blue and the grass is green. And they say it's just greener on the other side. Well, ha-ha to that! I know there is science backing everything, but I just believe that if someone really wants to think that, then they could.

I was one of those people once. I lived in a small town. Worked in a clothing store. Had lots of friends and went out all the time. Dinner, movies, clubs—really enjoyed my life. Worked 60 hours a week owning my own store. I really enjoyed that, too, it kept me busy.

I had two other people working for me. Sally and Chris; those two were great. We had so much fun together. Sally is married and has two children Kayti and John. Her husband's name is Al. He is a doctor; my doctor to be exact. Very sweet guy and a big flirt, too. Chris is gay, but a very good dresser. He can sweet-talk anyone into buying clothes, even if they didn't show any interest in the clothes, at all. He gave me the best tips of all. Especially this one time I had to go on a date. Chris really helped me out. I had nothing to wear that night and I was going to a very fancy restaurant. Chris came to my rescue that night; he came over and put together an outfit that was absolutely 'to die for.' These are two people I miss very much right now. It's hard sitting in this room and wondering if it was all-to-real or if it was an illusion. I guess that's why I am here, to figure out everything.

As I sit here, I think of why Jane (me, myself) is actually here. I am going to have to start at the time when my friend Lynn and I went on a trip. We had decided to go to Canada for a few days. Just to get out, away from our boring town, and the people we see day in and day out. On the way, we stopped and stayed in a couple of towns. Lynn and I have been friends ever since I could remember. We went to preschool together and graduated from High School together. I knew her like the back of my hand. Just to tell you what she looked like, she had long, blonde hair and, to sum it all up, had a 36-26-36 figure. Every man's dream!

Whenever I would stop places with her, every guy would look at her. Not that they didn't look at me, but I guess I just have to say simply that I am just ordinary looking. Not quite a size three, more like a size seven. No blonde hair, but beautiful, brown hair. I admit it, she's beautiful and very fun to be with. Well, on with the story about our trip.

We had stopped at this one bar and decided to get something to eat. When we walked in, we grabbed a table near the bar. We noticed two very cute guys staring at us. They wanted to buy us a drink, we told them that we just stopped in here to eat lunch, and then we were on our way.

"Where are you headed," cute guy number one said.

"Why do ya even need to know," I replied back.

"Be nice to these wonderful men that are going to buy us lunch," said Lynn.

"Oh, we offered the drinks and now you expect us to buy you lunch," cute guy number two said. That conversation lasted all night long, we were having so much fun.

We ended up getting our lunch and drinks for free. And a lot more things happened that night. When we finally arrived in Canada, we went to Old Fort Williams and Niagara Falls. The best part of it was we got our first tattoo together. Lynn had gotten a butterfly and I had gotten a rose.

So the years had past and Lynn became a Hair Stylist. And as I had told you before, I owned my own clothing store. Thinking back again on these times, we had gone on *so* many shopping trips together—to London, and then, a year later, to Las Vegas. We have definitely had our fun in the past. We were two peas in a pod. One night we went out to a particular Club. She had met a guy named Larry there. After that night, I didn't see much of her for a few years. I got a call one night from Lynn telling me she is going to get married to Larry. She wanted me to be the Maid of Honor. Well, of course, I told her yes.

Her wedding turned out to be the most beautiful wedding I have ever seen. There were roses everywhere, in our hair, in our bouquets, on the pews of the church. They had written their own vows to each other. When Lynn began to say her vows to Larry, I lost it. I cried through the rest of the wedding.

Well, a year latter they had a baby boy. They named him Teddy. When Lynn was little she had an obsession with teddy bears. So, that is why she named him Teddy; also, it suited him, because he was a ten-pound baby.

When I look at the three of them I can honestly say that they have a great family. He owns his own restaurant now with a guy named Nick. They grew up together and they have been trying to set me up with him. Their food is elegant and nothing but Italian served there.

"It's eight o' clock lights out," Jack said. Well, I guess that means that I am done writing for tonight. It's a little hard to write in the dark. And just like clockwork at five a.m. in the morning the lights are turned on.

We all have chores that we have to do here, and mine is gardening. I just keep to myself around here—everyone else is crazy. There's this one guy that washes all the dishes in this place, by hand, everyday. And he hits himself every ten minutes. There's a girl that does nothing but cuts up paper into little pieces like confetti. When people do leave this place we get to use it for celebrating.

After Lynn had her baby, we began to hang out more. She would visit me at work and we would have a blast together, even though we couldn't go on our trips anymore to far-away places. We would always have Teddy with us wherever we would go. He was a really great baby to take places. He hardly ever cried and he ate all the time.

Lynn was also trying to set me up with Nick again. He's really cute, but he is *so* stuck on himself I can't stand it. You know the big and strong type. Lynn and I would watch movies and eat pizza twice a week at her house.

I just think her husband is *so* cute. He just showers her with gifts all the time. For instance Lynn tells me herself that she gets jewelry, flowers and clothes from him. Whenever I see them together, she treats him like dirt. She yells at him in front of company. Cuts him down constantly about not helping around the house more. And I never saw her even once thank him for anything. She takes him for granted very much. Which reminds me of a poem I wrote a few years ago. I guess it shows how greedy she had become and how she came across to me. She is my best friend, but I thought it suited her.

Little kid in a candy Store

As his eyes grow bigger
His hands reach out
Too many to taste
Too many in sight

One is black
One is brown
He can't decide
So many colors
So many are good

The black is tangy, but sweet
The brown is chalky, but good
But the orange color is the one

He went home with so many

As he sat on his chair, He popped
One by one and continued
Until they were all gone
But that didn't hit him just right
He wanted more and more

So he went back

> He took the yellow, white and
> Pink ones, too
> He continued to eat one by one
>
> I guess that still wasn't enough
> He went on for days and days and days

If he's not busting his butt off at work, he is spending every waking moment with her and Teddy. He has no free time for himself, unless he is out buying her a gift of some sort. I never see him while I am at their house; he's always working on those nights. I usually see him when we all get together for our work meetings at his restaurant.

Chris and Sally are so much fun to be with. Sometimes it's hard for Sally to go out with us, because of her kids and everything. But Chris, on the other hand, is game for just about anything that fly's in front of his face.

We would always get together and discuss new ways in selling and merchandising. Also, it would always be open for us to discuss our personal lives. I believe that one should always come to work happy; if not I would like to know what is bothering them. Then I would know why their work habits changed.

That night we discussed how other businesses are doing around us. I would always send Chris to spy on the other stores; he was always such a sly spy. No one even suspected him of working in a clothing store. Another reason why I always liked going there is to see Larry bust his cute butt at work. The way his restaurant was laid out was one-half restaurant the other a bar.

After our meeting was over, I would always stay and play a game of darts with Larry. I would always have this feeling he would stare at my butt when it was my turn to throw. Lynn never knew about us playing darts together; I was very afraid of her getting mad at me. We were very close friends, so I didn't want to say anything that would ruin our friendship. I didn't want her to think I was trying to steal her husband right from under her feet.

One year had passed; Lynn and I did the same things every week. We talked about the same problems. Then one day she seemed trapped inside herself, lost and not quite sure about what to do. Through our conversations and fights with each other, I think I finally figured her out. I believe she's jealous of Larry being successful an' all. She only works at the salon part time. She was completely jealous of her husband.

I still went to the restaurant to have our meeting with Chris and Sally, but I believe I was more obsessed with Larry. Like a High School crush; but always afraid to go up to the guy and actually say that you like him. I guess I didn't tell you what Larry looked like.

He was 6'2" with brown hair, brown eyes and a body that would knock you right over every time you would look at it. And, of course, our weekly dart game was still on, followed by the best conversations of Lynn and Larry. We had talked about their problems more and more. I guess I didn't want to say too much, I just told him what I knew and that was it. I had left it brief because Lynn was still my friend and I had felt bad doing that behind her back.

Well, back to my gardening, again. This is the one thing that keeps me sane in this place. Hey, to tell you what I just found out around here—a woman in her forties jabbed herself with a pencil. Today Jack told me that she was doing so well that she was going to get out of here in five months. She has been here for almost 20 years now and doesn't want to leave. She came here for killing her baby. She couldn't live with herself, and didn't want to face the 'real' world.

"So, that's why," I had said to Jack.

"No, that is *not* the only reason," he had told me.

He explained to me that her husband had been beating her very badly for many years. The last time the guy took a bat to her and started wailing on her. At that time she was holding her baby in her arms to protect it. She had started squeezing her baby tighter and tighter because of the pain of the bat wailing on her, and she had suffocated it to death. The people told her that it wasn't her fault.

They had sent her here in fear of her harming herself because of what had happened, and to let her heal from her injures. When she came here she told all of them that it really was her fault! Nothing would have happened to her baby if she had left long before it had ever happened. She told Jack she would never forgive herself for what had happened.

"Poor lady," I had told Jack.

How could she ever forgive herself—I guess I wouldn't have. But I wouldn't harm myself either! My food has finally arrived—rice and an egg roll.

Lynn had called me the next day and told me she thought her husband was cheating on her. I had asked her why she thought that way. What gave her that idea? She had told me that Larry has been acting funny some nights when he comes home. He doesn't sit down and talk about his day anymore with her. He doesn't even ask about Teddy; and before this he would.

"Did Teddy do anything funny today?" he would usually say.

She told me that he didn't even pay attention to her anymore; he would just come home, sit and read the paper. I had told her that she was over-reacting. All married couples go through that. Sally and her husband go through that all the time. Sally told me it's just that they have been together for a while and need to go out by themselves without their two kids always being there. You need your time to just be you.

But really, the whole time I was thinking that she is selfish and always thinking of herself, and not putting her husband's needs into the picture. I also thought she might have been talking about *me*, so I didn't want her to get any ideas. That same night Larry had asked me to go to Italy with him so he could visit restaurants and could get ideas about his own.

Well, that's just a whole other story. A few weeks had passed and I still didn't know what to say to him. So, one night the three of us went to our meeting at the restaurant. We were discussing a new line of clothing for our store. I was thinking of going with a certain color theme—basic colors, colors that would go with anything. We were tossing around gray, black, white, blue, red, pink, and some other colors of which we weren't quite sure.

Larry had come up to me and told me to meet him in his office in a few minutes. I looked at Chris then Sally and wasn't sure on what to do. They had told me to go—what's it going to hurt? So, when my few minutes were up I went into his office.

When I walked in he asked me, "So, what's your answer on the trip to Italy?"

I didn't say anything for a while, in my long, disgusting silence. He began to smile at me. When he does smile it's a good one!

So, I smiled back and said, "YES, YES, YES, I will go with you to Italy! When are we leaving?" He told me not to tell Lynn about this and to get myself packed because we were leaving in a couple of days.

I then shouted, "WOW, that soon? Give me a couple of days to think about it."

He told me, "I will give you until tomorrow."

He then told me that I was the only one that could go with him; his wife had to stay home with Teddy. Nick had to watch their business while he was gone, and we would only be gone for a three days.

I had gone home that night and thought about it. I thought about what I would be doing to my best friend and then how it could be better for my own business. I also have never been to Italy before. But not to share this with my best friend would kill me. I know, I think he's cute, hot, sexy and good enough to eat. But how, how would I pull this off? I couldn't tell her that I was going to stay with my parents.

They had passed away when I was twenty years old. They were so in love with each other, but also in so much fear of one another dying and leaving each other alone, that they patiently waited until I was old enough and was set in what I was going to do with my life. Then one night they had overdosed with sleeping pills. They left their handwritten will on the side of their bed. The will stated that I was to get all of their worldly possessions. After, I sold their house, and this is how I bought my business.

Well, back to how I would tell Lynn I will be leaving

town for a couple of days. And then a light bulb turned on in my head. I will tell her that Chris, from work, is having a problem, a family problem, and that I am the only one he trusted in his life. He hasn't told his parents that he is gay, yet. He really has, but *that* is what I am going to tell Lynn.

Chapter Two

Well, a week has passed. Larry and I are on our way to Rome, Italy. It is going to be so much fun. Restaurants, shopping—and more restaurants and shopping. I didn't really know how Larry felt, but I was going to have the–absolutely–most fun you could ever have on a trip. He told me when he had gotten the tickets that he had put 'Mr. and Mrs.' on them. He told me, also, that he got them at a discount this way.

While we were talking on the plane, he told me that no one knows that he even was going with anyone on this trip. We then talked about their relationship together, how he felt and how she felt towards him. Then he asked me about my life. I had told him it was as boring as watching someone fly-fish for a couple of hours.

"Maybe someday, but just not today," I said, afraid of putting him to sleep. I also told him that I have never had a long-term relationship with anyone, so I just might not be the one to answer all his questions.

He replied, "Well, who do you want me to talk with, Nick?"

"Of course not. I wouldn't even put you through the torture of having to ask Nick anything." I said.

So, we ended up talking about the two of them the whole time. I found myself day-dreaming a little bit. I really didn't want to end up talking about this the whole time.

We finally arrived in Rome and had taken a cab to our hotel. Larry went to get our rooms. When I walked up to him, he then told me that there was only one room available for us. It had a queen size bed and a sofa sleeper. I agreed to take the room as long as I got the bed. Our hotel was called the Colonna Palace Hotel. It did, indeed, look like a palace to me.

When Larry and I got to our room to get settled in, I found myself still a little wired from the flight. The plane ride was long, but our conversation was pretty invigorating at times, and I didn't really want to sit in this room the rest of the night.

We then decided to go down to the cocktail lounge of the Hotel and have ourselves a drink. Besides, I was still very nervous about being here with him. He hadn't made a move on me yet, and I really wasn't sure I wanted him to. I was just thinking of what it would be like.

When we finally sat down and started talking to each other. I wasn't thinking of Lynn anymore. We started to talk about the paintings on the walls and what our lives would be like if we were in that particular painting—riding in a boat along the river, reading poetry to each other.

I mentioned that I have written poetry and I am still working on some every now and again. It's coming slowly to me, but I know, eventually, I will have a lot written. Larry wanted me to tell him one poem.

I couldn't really think of one, but I did remember one that I had written a long time ago. I told him I had written it on one of the trips that I had taken with his wife. We stopped at a beach once, and, while she was sun bathing, I was watching the people and kids play.

So, I told him this poem –

A DAY AT THE BEACH

As the light gleams, off the brown sand

And the little feet march, as fast as they can

As the ocean screams, their arms wave free

And the buckets accumulate, as fast as a little bee

As their piles grow larger, the day becomes darker

And that would make it time,

to end the journey of the poor little Parker

I told him I would tell him more at a later date.

He asked me, "How do you even think of writing poems?"

"I guess the words just fly right out of me, onto the paper. I don't really think about it. It just comes to me," I said.

Our drinks had become more intense now, as had our conversation with each other. The night grew long and we gradually became tired. We ended up walking back to our room. I wasn't even remotely nervous, now that I had a few drinks in me. Larry had been a complete gentleman to me this night and I thanked him for that. That night, as I lay in my bed and with Larry on the sofa, I was happy that the day had ended so well.

The next day I awoke for breakfast. Larry was already up and ready to go hunting for fresh and new ideas. I told him to go without me today, so I could freshen up this morning. Just before he walked out the door, he bent down and gave me a kiss on the cheek, and then thanked me for such a wonderful night. When he left, I just smiled about the kiss—it was very nice. I went to get ready and there was a knock at the door. I was wondering who would even be knocking at my door, so I answered as I was throwing my robe on in the process. It was just some guy with a box. I thanked him and went on inside.

There was no name on the box, so I opened it. There were three red roses inside, and I thought, 'Wow, he didn't have to do this for me.' Then I saw the card, opened it and read the message, 'To my beloved Larry, whom I miss so very much.' I thought to myself, whatever. What am I even doing here since they love each other so much? This was my best friend that I was defying our friendship.

This was so unlike me to be doing this—not that anything has happened yet—or will ever happen on this trip. Larry and I are just really good friends—just like Lynn and I are really good friends. But I had questioned myself a lot—why am I even here? I had put the box back together, finished getting ready and went to get my *cappuccino* and *cornetto*.

Larry wasn't back yet, so I headed out to look at the stores. I walked out on the streets of Rome. The clothes here were well displayed and the people were very helpful. The order and the way they had displayed the clothes were fantastic. I was walking around for a couple of hours and thought that it was time for me to go back to the hotel. I also heard that there were more shops south of us, but that they were more expensive. I had gotten really good deals in the stores that I had shopped in today. When I got back, Larry was in the room. I asked him if he had gotten the box and he said, "Yes, but I threw them out."

I wondered why he would even do such a thing. Larry then told me that he was still mad at her for always yelling at him. He had done nothing wrong. Well, at that moment he told me that she accused him of sleeping around, again. That was the day he left for Italy. So, that is why he didn't want them or even want to look at them. This was a very bitter side of him that I had not seen before.

Larry felt like spending some money and had noticed a really expensive restaurant to take me. I didn't really have anything nice to wear. He mentioned to me that I should just go to the store and buy the most expensive dress I could find. I had asked him how I was ever going to pay for it and he had told me to just charge it on my credit card. He will pay it off when I receive the bill in the mail.

So I walked down to the store and found just a simple, A-line, black dress—but a very elegant one. I also knew I could wear this one again. I got back to the room and slipped on the dress. He had already brought his best-looking suit with him. I asked him if he thought we were going out somewhere special. He had said that it never hurts to be prepared in any situation.

We walked to dinner that night. When we arrived, there was a table already done up with rose petals scattered on the table and heart shaped candles burning in the middle. I asked him if he had done all of this.

"Of course! I wanted this to be a special night for a special friend of mine," Larry said.

I felt like crying tears of enjoyment. Just to think that a very good friend of mine wanted to do that for me. What would my lover, when I do get one, do for me, as well? We began to order. I ordered *Penne Arabiata* and Larry ordered Spaghetti *Alle Vongole*.

Our night was so much fun; Larry had tried to tell them that we were both from a newspaper, back home. He thought that we might have gotten a free meal this way, but instead they gave us a free desert. He then told me that I looked very beautiful tonight. He mentioned that even though the dress is very plain looking, it flattered me very well. My face turned red with such a compliment given to me.

I began to think that I have had relationships in the past but none that has put me under such a spell. I almost felt like I was drugged and floating on top of a cloud with bubbles surrounding me. His deep, dark-brown eyes were *so* beautiful. He has huge arms and big hands, and, wow, everything about him just makes me melt. That night felt very romantic for me. Right then I really wished I were with him.

We went on a long walk that night after dinner. I learned that Rome has five special walks and we walked for three hours around the third one, which was called, *Il Piazza Navona*. We saw *Via Dei Gigli D'Oro* (street of golden lilies), with its many marble sculptures. I think one was called *Via Dei Soldati*. I wasn't quite sure if it was a lion or a bear.

We saw so many buildings that night. When we finally got back to the hotel room, he gave me a big hug and reached his hand behind me, placed it on the back of my head, pulled me closer to him and gave me a big kiss. I didn't know what to do. My arms flopped along my side, my knees went weak, and the kiss felt like an eternity.

Larry then thanked me for the most wonderful night he has ever had. I then asked him a question. I didn't even know why I did. I shouldn't have, but I asked him about Lynn, and if he had ever, in his life, had such a wonderful night with her. He gave me this strange look, as if I were cooked meat and should be eaten now. I then suddenly burst out and apologized to him. I knew how upset he was and I shouldn't have even said her name. Larry had said it was fine that I had said her name, and he is not going to be mad at me. He was wondering why that even popped into my head, especially after the best kiss he's ever had. I told him that I was sure he had a kiss such as that one from another woman.

He said, "Sadly, no; I haven't until now."

I was his *first* best kiss. I just began to cry; he asked me why I crying. He sat me down on the bed and then sat right beside me. I told him that it was because I was having such a good time that I didn't want this to end. He told me that he didn't want it to end, either, and said that it was getting late. We ended up going to bed. That night I told him he could sleep in the same bed as me and he did. Nothing happened that night, other then fighting over the blanket while we were sleeping.

The next day I awoke and he was gone. There was a note on the pillow beside me along with a red rose, which read, "I went to visit other restaurants today and will be back later tonight…just to enjoy one last night with the best friend I could have in the whole world."

He also said for me to go out and enjoy myself shopping today. Well, I couldn't really pass that up, now. I took another long bath this morning before I went shopping for the day.

I had so much fun, and I decided to walk the main shopping streets today. This began at the foot of the Spanish steps. The street name is *Via Condotti*, south along the *Via Del Corso*, and which had the biggest fashion names—Gucci, Valentino, Cartier, and more. I had walked into a couple of jewelry stores and, of course, it was very desirable. On the streets of *Via Borgognona* and *Missoni*, there's an Armani. I could go on and on about the designers and the clothes they have. I wish I could live here and have this life. Seven hours later I was back at the hotel. I walked into the room with both of my arms full of bags. Then I walked over to the bed and plopped down, I was so tired. I don't know how people do it. I suppose they're used to it, by now. I then looked over at the pillow after seeing something in the corner of my eye. It had been another note from Larry to me.

It read, "Slip on something sexy, and meet me in the hotel bar."

I threw on my new black Gucci pantsuit and my new Gucci heals to go with it. Then I took my time getting to the bar. I thought to myself, 'He can wait for me.' I noticed him sitting at a table in the corner of the bar sipping his drink. I watched him for a while gazing at everyone in the bar—more like studying them, looking at what they wore and how they treated each other. I walked up and said, "What's up?" really loudly to scare him. It had worked; he jumped so high into the air that they could almost peel him off the ceiling. We laughed for a while about that and then he got all-serious on me.

He looked into my eyes and said, "Jane, I love you, and I have loved you with all my heart for awhile, now."

He told me that he wanted to get a divorce now and has been thinking about it. Not just because of me, but everything put together. I asked him if he was forgetting someone in his life, like Lynn and his son, Teddy. Larry then told me that he would talk to her when he got back.

We walked around the streets of Rome for a while. We

had long, deep conversations about what we should do. We thought about our lives together, and owning our own business, going on business trips together, and looking out for the competition.

We thought of what our love would be like with each other—no arguing or even getting mad about the house. We wouldn't live with each other right away. Then we thought about him staying with Lynn and trying to work it out between them. I told him that I knew Lynn loved him very much, but is just a little jealous of him and the business.

Then I told him that maybe we shouldn't do anything, just yet. We should wait while he tried to work things out with Lynn. We should just relax and enjoy the rest of the night with each other. We then began to hold each other's hands while we were walking.

This wasn't even close to being our small town back in the U.S. There, everyone stuck their nose in where it didn't belong and everyone even knew each other's names. I was thinking to myself that it would be nice to live here for a while, but not forever, because I would miss my friends a little too much. Sitting here, we watched everyone go home for lunch to spend time with his or her family. It is the most family-orientated place, ever.

This was our last night with each other and I didn't want it to end. This trip made me realize that I love Larry more then anything. But I can't believe I did this to Lynn, or, for that matter, even doing it to myself. I knew it wouldn't be easy to be with him for the rest of my life so why did I even try.

Our plane leaves in the morning, and I should get some rest. All I have to do is close my eyes and fall asleep; Larry is already asleep next to me in the bed. I just thought of all the fun we shared together these past couple of days and fell right to sleep.

It was now six a.m. in the morning. We are heading back to our small town and try to act as if nothing happened. I didn't know what to say to him. I wasn't going to tell Lynn anything. Larry agreed to keep quiet for a while and we would just see what fell in our path.

We arrived that night and I hid, because Lynn was here to pick Larry up from the airport. I then saw them hugging and giving each other kisses. It made me furious to see even that. After they left, I grabbed a taxi and went home. I sat up for half the night going through everything that just happened. It blows me away that he was such a good kisser and that he even told me that he loved me. I didn't know what to think, and writing always makes me feel a lot better, so I sat down and began to write a poem about what had happened.

Love in your eyes

For every glance and gleam
I saw in your eyes
I found a beam
That was filled with lies

Besides what happened
It needs to be forgotten

Because every smile you gave me
Made the sun come up
Like our coffee
Every morning in our cup

You made my spirits feel alive
Like bubbles floating along the side

    Well, here it is. I typed it on a piece of paper and put it into my purse.

Coreen Picconatto

Chapter Three

I told Jack that I started writing again. He stole a flashlight for me to use at night. They don't have a camera in the room where I am. So, if I hide it well enough I can start writing at night. Well, to let you know what's up around this place, this other guy, who helps me do the gardening on the other side of this building, had a heart attack. I asked Jack if he was going to be all right. He told me that the man was in intensive care, right now. He is a very strong willed man, and that, yes, Jack thought he would do all right. But now I was stuck doing his part of the gardening as well; well, that's okay, I will try my best. That is an unfortunate thing to have happened; I would never want it to happen to me.

I wrote a letter to the warden so see if I could have my walls painted. I was sick of looking at the same color day-in and day-out. He wrote me a letter back saying that everyone else has to have the same color in his or her room, so 'no.'

Jack and I talked today for a while about life.
He had said that by him working here, it has not made him crazier; it has made him very insightful.
He sees more about how people think. Just to let you know, Jack is my sexy consoler. He also told me that he didn't get me the flashlight, because he liked me. He had gotten it for me because he believed in me. He told me that since he has been meeting with me I have never appeared happier, then I did right now. He believes that the writing helps me, and he wants to help me as much as he can.

So I asked him, "Does that mean that I will be getting out of this place soon?"

He said, "Until you admit what you have done wrong, you will not get even remotely close to being gone from this place."

He told me that it wasn't his place to tell me what went wrong. That was something that I had to figure out myself.

The next day when I got back to the store I had called Sally and asked her how it went. She told me that Lynn had called once, but then she remembered that I was with Chris. But, other then that, the business went really well. Sally knew I went to Italy, so she covered for me. She asked me how my trip went. I didn't really know what to tell her, so I told her I had the time of my life. I shopped to my heart's content. We had gone out to eat at fancy restaurants on the nights that we were there. I told Sally that one night he even kissed me. I thought I heard her mouth drop on the other side of the phone.

Then she screamed, "What? Did I miss something, did you do anything else?"

I told her that nothing else happened, other than that he told me that he loved me and he wanted to divorce Lynn.

"Tell me that you told him that you *didn't* want him to get a divorce."

"Yes, I told him that I wanted him to wait and just see what happens next," I replied.

Sally didn't know what to say to me, other then she thought that Lynn should be told what happened. I told her that it would ruin everything, and I would lose her as a very good friend. I thought that it was just Italy, because it was such a beautiful city and, maybe, it made us do things. It was as if it put us under a spell.

Sally said that she had to go, but she would talk to me more when she comes to work.

I had already told the sob-story to Chris the night before. He was very excited for me for having such a good time. Chris is so different about things. He looks at life as an adventure and thinks people should make the most of it. Time has passed and it was time for Sally to walk in. Just then she positively flew through the door, walked right past me and gave me *the look*. It's like your mother coming in to yell at you. She went straight back and changed. When she walked out of the back room she came right out and said it, "You shouldn't keep this secret from Lynn. The longer you wait the longer it will eat you up inside."

She knew me; she knew what I was like. Things like that bother me more than anything else. She had been thinking and had told me that she remembered Larry and I at the restaurant, giving each other looks and waving. She always thought that we were just really good friends and nothing more. I told her that I agreed, but something happened along the way that we couldn't help. It just happened and pulled us closer to each other. I guess I knew it was there, but never really wanted to admit it to myself. I think it was because of me being friends with Lynn.

Sally asked me, "How are you even going to face her when you go over to her house?" Especially when I *am* in love with her husband. I know it going to be extremely hard, but I will just have to try. I was going to wait one more day before I even called her. I had to think more about this made-up trip I supposedly took with Chris. I said my 'good-byes' to Sally and went on home. I just didn't want to talk about it anymore. The rest of the day and night I had just vegged out in front of the TV and watched my shows.

I awoke the next morning on my couch, thinking that this was the day to have our meeting at the restaurant. I knew in my heart that I shouldn't really go. I also had to call Lynn today and tell her that I was back—and tell her a lie about my visit to Chris's parent's house. Needless to say, I haven't heard from Larry, either. I still had the poem I wrote in my purse. I decided that we all would go to the restaurant and have our meeting that day. I had called Chris at the store, because he had opened it. I told him to give Sally a call because we are going to have our meeting tonight at the restaurant as scheduled.

Chris screamed with enjoyment, "I am so excited about you seeing Larry."

I had told him to 'calm yourself down, that it's just going to be a meeting; I am not going to talk to him.

I had told no one about the poem I had written. I want it to be a surprise. That day I also called Lynn to tell her that I was back. She was thrilled to hear from me. So I knew she didn't know about the trip or even about Larry and I. She had asked me how it went about telling Chris's parents about him being gay. I told her that his parents didn't even seem to care. They figured as much anyway. They told me that he has never had a girlfriend, and he's always talking about fashion. So they just figured he was and was waiting for him to say something to them about it. And, also, being such a good-looking kid and all, he's more likely to be gay. I had thought his parents were very cool and laid-back, kind of like Chris.

Lynn was happy it went so well. Then she told me that Larry had a great time on his trip. I said, that's right he went on a trip, how was it for him. She told me that he had went to fifteen different restaurants and brought back three books. She mentioned that he knew a lot more now and was going to change his menu. She also said that the trip helped him out a lot. I had told her that I thought this was really great. I then told her that I was going to have a meeting there tonight and I would check-out the new items. She told me to have lots of fun and said, 'good bye.'

That night the three of us got together at the restaurant and started out with the famous 'soup and salad.' I also ordered a new item on the menu. Sally was looking around the place, and looking pretty obvious who she was looking for. She then leaned over and said that Lynn was here.

I burst out, "What! Why in the world is she here. She should be home taking care of Teddy."

Sally told me to calm down, she said that you know it's her restaurant, too. "Yeah, Yeah, I know I shouldn't have even come here."

Chris said, "Just because things change, it doesn't mean you should change." I know I have a right to be here, too. I then looked over and saw the both of them kissing. My eyes began to water; I didn't really know what to think. I told myself that I wasn't going to cry, and I am not going to cry! I sucked it up and then began to talk about business again. We talked about Italy and the stores along the *Via Codotti*, the clothes, and just how fabulous they were, the city, and just how fantastic and romantic it was.

It was as if I was in a dream, and that reality was a figment of my imagination, just like the preserved art and sculptures. Just then I had realized that it was the city which put me under that spell, of floating on a cloud. I was dreaming the whole time, none of this happened. Sally then told me that Lynn was leaving. I then got a huge smile on my face. Just then I knew that Larry had already noticed me. He did the manly nod and winked. I returned his friendly gesture with a smile from cheek to cheek.

We continued to work the rest of the night. I still was thinking about all that had happened this past week. I just thought work was more important right now. When we were all done with our meeting, Chris and Sally left. Sally said that I shouldn't do anything drastic tonight. I then went to say good-bye to Larry. I told him it was nice to see you again.

"Wait!" Larry said with an anxious voice. He had wanted to talk to me about Italy. I had told him it was fun while it lasted, but I am going home now.

"Everything that I told you in Italy is true," he said to me while my back was facing him.

"I do love you, but I just can't act on it now because Lynn would take Teddy away from me and I just couldn't stand that."

He told me that he has to figure some things out right now. My eyes began to water again. I reached into my purse and threw the poem at him.

"Read it when I am gone," I had told him.

He told me that he understood and waited until I had left the room to read it. But I had forgotten my jacket in his office. I walked back in and Larry was crying. I never before saw a man cry. I didn't know what to do, so I went up to him and gave him a great big hug.

When I had leaned down to hug him, he had grabbed me closer with his big strong arms and on to his lap I fell. I didn't know what to say I just waited as I was still sitting on his lap. His head turned and he began to get closer to me. He looked into my eyes as we were face to face. He then kissed me, and everything became clear again. I felt the tingle in my stomach and then got up off his lap.

I looked at him and was lost in words. I turned around and walked out of the room, hopped into my car and went home. I then cracked open a beer and ran my bath water. As I was sitting on the side of the tub, I was thinking to myself, 'Everything happens for a reason. There is a reason why we love each other.' When I slipped into the tub, I had a pen in one hand and a notebook in the other. I wrote another poem about life.

Everyday

On every star, there's a moon
On every moon, there's a sun

For everyday the sun shines
There's a tree, waving at me

For every drop of rain
There's a cloud, with a smile

For every day a leaf would fall
We would find, some kid kicking the ball

For every day we see snow
And think, Wow! The white stuff can glow

For every day we hit zero below
We vision—a hot cup would be a great decision

Just remember

To whom you may see
There's another just like me

After I wrote that I thought to myself, there's more in life then Larry. If I can't have him, I will just look at the brighter side of things. No matter what happens in life, there is always a way to look at it differently. For instance, I looked at my parent's death as a good thing. They had always loved me and showed me how much they cared for me. They showed me that they loved each other more than anything else in life—that it is okay to die, and that I shouldn't be afraid of it.

I had taken a couple days off from writing and worked more on my gardening. My bulbs are starting to bloom. Tulips are my favorite—the yellow ones especially. When I visit with Jack, he always wants me to tell him how my writing is coming. But I'm not quite sure how to say it. I had told him before that it was coming very well and that I am still writing before I go to bed. Besides, it helps me sleep better.

Jack can be so serious sometimes about life. He said that I must keep on writing, it's the only way. I told him that I am not sure if I can figure out why I am here. I told him that I would try with all of my heart.

There's a lot that Jack doesn't tell me about my life. He just wants me to figure it out on my own. I am here and I don't even know why; all I know is that everyone thinks I was crazy when I walked in here. Well, I guess I am back to writing about my life. One thing about this is that I remember things as I began to write them, as long as I am not thinking about why, and just writing, it comes back to me.

Wow! The sun was really bright the next day. It was brighter than normal, and I thought something might have happened. I also thought about what had happened the night before. Whether or not I should have said more to him or even just kissed him one more time. No, I guess that would have been asking for too much. Before I opened the store, I was sorting out papers and my mind wandered. I thought of another poem. It just popped in my head like wild fire. I wrote it down on paper, of course, and I was therefore late in opening the store.

One Apple Left

To look at something so red and divine

As the watery substance in your mouth develops

You stop and think

They all have there own shape and texture

Every way you look at it, it develops a new personality

But still, deep in the back of your mind, you want it

You have had one in the past,

But not one that looks quite likes this

Just the thought of that first initial crunch,

And something running down the corner of your mouth

Is irresistible, but you can't

So, it lies on that old windowsill

Rotting in despair

When I walked in the front of the store, it was a disaster. Then I remembered we had our meeting last night. I think I might change the restaurant to which we go. I was thinking of Chinese food next. I guess now that I know he has feelings for me, I really can't see him anymore. I was so stressed-out that day I just rearranged the entire store. Well, it's not so busy when it's cold out. I get my business in the summer. I paid my bills from the money I had gotten from my summer business. It's not as if I need clothes anyway. It's my company, so I helped myself all the time and just wrote it off, later.

It was so nice to feel wanted again. But I had made my decision; I will not see him again. That night when I came home I heard a message on my machine to call Lynn, so I did. When she answered she was crying. I asked her what was wrong—something with Teddy, Larry, what was wrong? All she did was cry. I thought she knew.
 I asked anyway, "Is there something I could help you with."
 She said, "I don't think anyone can help me."
 She told me that she was all screwed up, and then she asked me over to the house. Of course, I said, 'yes, I would be right over.' When I arrived at her house, her eyes were very puffy from crying, but she seemed to be doing better.
 I asked her, "What could I do to help her feel better?"
 Lynn just started to ramble on and on about Larry and

how he's here for her, but then he isn't. She feels that when he looks at her that he just looks right through her. He answers Lynn's questions and plays with Teddy, but that his mind is somewhere else. It's as if he can't smile anymore. She had told me that it must be a woman in his life. I asked her how she could believe such a lie. Larry is a good man and all she has to do is ask him if anything is wrong.

Lynn looked at me and laughed in my face. She didn't see how that was even possible. She told me that when he comes home all he does is play with Teddy or cook. He doesn't pay attention to her and her needs anymore. He never helps around the house. I told her just to talk to him about it; maybe he would like to help you out and tell you why he seems so lifeless and distant.

I had told her that if she gave up when things got tough that her marriage wouldn't last long at all. She had to be strong and fight for what she has—right now. I stressed to her not to give up on her and Larry, that Teddy needs both of them, right now more than ever.

Chapter Four

Jack told me that I was getting distant again. He wanted to know why I was so sad. I told him that I was getting really sick of not knowing how I ended up in this place. He told me that I am the only one person who can answer that question. I asked him if I was injured or sick? Did I mumble any words when I came here? He told me that I wasn't ready for that yet, it would ruin me and I wouldn't be able to write anymore. I guess that he is right; I probably wouldn't be able to write if I knew why I was here. Jack reads what I write so he knows everything that I have written.

He told me another story about what was going on around here—about this lady who tried to commit suicide, and tried to jump out of her window. She ran as fast as she could towards it and knocked herself unconscious. They found out later that she overdosed on the medication she was taking. It had calmed her down so much that she didn't even see the bars on her window. I felt bad for all of these people in here; half of them can't help themselves. It's really cute sometimes, too—there's this one guy that tells everyone that he loves him or her and wants the best for them. He just sits in his chair and says, "I love you" to anyone that walks by.

A week had passed and I had scheduled a meeting at the Chinese restaurant. When the three of us got together to have our meeting, Chris asked, "Why are we here? Shouldn't we be with your good friend, Larry?"

"Why should I do that? I have decided not to see him

anymore. Lynn is my friend and I don't want that to end, I replied."

I told them that I needed Lynn as my friend and Larry should not be the one to ruin that for me. I was needy and desperate to have someone to love. No one has ever been there for me as Larry has, except for you guys.

He has been a good friend and I am sorry to see that end. Our love for each other was purely a mistake. Sally then asked me why I was saying these things. It didn't sound like me at all. Then she asked me if something had happened that night when they left his restaurant and I had stayed to say good-bye.

I explained to them that we had kissed again and then I walked out. I didn't know what to do; I wanted him so badly. But I thought of Teddy and Lynn. Then I knew that I didn't want to ruin that for them. So, that is why I am never going to see him again. I will just have to see her when Larry is working his night shift. So we continued to talk business for the rest of the night.

When we got our check, our fortune cookies came along with it. That was my favorite part of the dinner. I began to open it and my fortune read, 'One small change today can create many big changes tomorrow.' I was really hoping *that* fortune would come true. But hoping for something is a really good start, I kept on telling myself.

Elasticity

> I put my love
> Through my hands
> To your heart and soul

I carry you
To the land
That is bright and bold

I have the strength
Of the bands
That will begin the hold.

Things went on the same for many weeks. I didn't see him or even talk to him on the phone. I would only go over to Lynn's house when he was working. My store stayed the same; I didn't change it around anymore. And we still went to the Chinese restaurant every time we had our meeting.

One night I remember going to our local bar. I was feeling like a beer that night. When I got there I noticed someone I knew in high school. It was Sam; he was my best friend in high school. I loved being with him; we would drive around for hours just talking about our life dreams, and what we wanted to do with them.

We went to the movies together and, of course, our famous bonfire parties. I then approached him; he looked down at me and said, 'hi,' as if he didn't even know who I was. I started to walk away and he grabbed my jacket and said he was sorry. I asked him if he knew who I was.

He said, "Of course, I know who my best bud in High School is."

I had asked him what he was up to, where does he lives now, why is he in town, is he married, any kids, what kind of job he had. He was telling me to slow down. We had grabbed a table and began to talk about what our life is like now. I told him that I own my business; clothing, of course. He piped up and said, "Of course, clothing." I have no love in my life and no dog, yet, either.

He told me that he is also alone. He has had no love in his life, yet. He is working for a big law firm in New York. I asked him, 'what are you doing there, are you a lawyer?' He said, 'Not yet, but he was a lawyer's assistant.' He is currently in school trying to become a lawyer. He was never a bright one in school. He was the guy that always cracks jokes in the back of the class, and trips up the smart ones. He was a simple goof-off and nothing more.

After we had all graduated from High School he just split, no good-bye or anything. I asked him about that, what had happened, and why he just took off like that. He told me that he had gotten caught up in a couple of things and that's it. He didn't really want to talk about it with me. I said to him that it was up to him. He doesn't have a dog yet, either. I asked him if he wanted to dance with me.

He told me, "Of course I would, honey. Nothing would give me more pleasure."

I told him, "You just swept me off my feet."

"What are you doing out alone, anyway?"

I told him that I just broken up with someone and I needed a drink.

We just kept on dancing and talking with each other. We were having so much fun together that I didn't want this to end. I offered him to come over to my house and he did. We sat up all night, just looking at old photos and yearbooks together.

"I had so much fun tonight," I told him.

"I had a lot of fun with you tonight, too."

"Do you want to come upstairs with me to my bedroom," I asked.

"Sure, I would love to sleep with you."

"No, we will wait, I just want you to lay in bed with me and hold me all night long."

"Of course I will. I'm sorry, I didn't mean for it to come out that way."

"That's okay, I didn't really take it in bad way, either."

So we went upstairs and slept all night long holding each other. It was so nice to have someone there to give you comfort and company. I told myself, that I need to find someone, quick, to be my husband and then I will have someone here to hold me forever.

Friends

>As we look back on our past
>We believe its gone fast
>
>As we find ourselves alone
>We just look over to our phone
>
>As on tear drops
>There's a hand with a Kleenex box
>
>As we reach our arms out
>There's a hug lurking about
>
>Just the sweet comfort
>Wipes away all our hurt

Friends are great to have, even if you haven't seen them in years. It seemed like fate that I ran into Sam that night. Just seeing his great big smile looking back at me while I was talking to him was a blessing to me. I know, now, that he was a great friend to me. Before he had left, he gave me a great big hug and a kiss on the cheek. Last night is just what I needed. A little dancing, a little talking. After my trip to Italy, that brought me back to reality. The affection, just him holding me in his arms, is what the doctor called for. I had gotten his address and phone number, so I could contact him anytime.

But he didn't really keep me from thinking of Larry, and his soft warm lips, his big arms and chest. He was like a huge, lovable teddy bear. I am not the one living with him, but I can't see how Lynn even remotely could get mad at him. I haven't seen her or even talked with her in awhile, but she must be doing okay.

I am regretting the idea I had not to see Larry. I am getting completely obsessive over him. It seems to me that no matter where I go—work, home, shower, car—or even what I do, he's in my mind. That's it—I can't take it. I am going to explode—just blast into little pieces. My primitive little life will be no more.

I am going to experiment on Larry with all of my options, starting right now. I need some exhilaration in my life, and not disappear when the simplest little thing happens to me. He kissed me, big deal. He's married; well, I'll get over that. Lynn, she just needs a good talking to. Maybe I will just ask her if she wants to go on a trip. I think I could find a way to let her know my situation with Larry. Sally was right; I need to tell her. Let her know how deep my feelings really are.

That night after work I went over to the restaurant to talk to Larry about my plan. He had to run a quick trip somewhere and he would be back real soon. As I waited at the bar for him, I had a couple Long Island Iced Teas. I just love that drink; they slide right down my throat. He then walked right through the door. He hadn't noticed me yet, but he was approaching the bar to put something away. He came straight over to me and ducked under behind the counter to put something on the bottom shelf. When he stood up again, we were staring each other face to face. He began to smile and then said, "Where have you been hiding? I haven't seen you in here, lately."

I asked him how he was doing and if everything was going well with Lynn. He had told me same things, there were just different days. I had asked him if that was a good thing or a bad thing. He didn't really answer me right away. I didn't really know how to react to that. I asked him if he was okay.

"What do you think? Lynn and I have had our differences, and now I love you. We can't be together. She would take Teddy away from me and I would never see him again. Of course you two wouldn't be friends anymore. So right now I have a big problem."

I then began to tell him about my plan to take Lynn on a trip with me to San Francisco. I told him that I would find a way to tell her when I am on this trip. But all we need to do is find someone to take care of Teddy while she is gone. He told me that wouldn't be a problem; he would take vacation time.

"I can't believe that you're okay with this plan,' I said. "I didn't really think that you would go for it."

"Of course. I guess right now I will do anything to be with you. I will try anything to find a way to divorce Lynn, he said."

"Okay, then. I will talk to Lynn tomorrow and set the date to go to San Francisco in a month. Until then we shouldn't be seen together."

We agreed on the deal and I went home.

Deceiving my friend is not me, but I am not going to sit around here and wait for the love of my life to drop from the sky. I am not going to be alone; I just can't be alone.

Alone

I'm all alone
I have nowhere to go
I have nowhere to hide

I'm all alone
I sit here and look at the sky

I'm all alone
I have nothing inside

I'm all alone
I have no love
I have no life

I'm all alone

So the next day I called Lynn and asked her if she wanted to take a trip with me. She asked me where, and I told her San Francisco. She was very excited, but said she had to ask Larry first and wondered who was going to take care of Teddy. I told her to call me back when she talks to her husband and finds out what's what. Just a few hours later she called me back and said that Larry was okay with her going. He was going to take a vacation when we go. I said great, and said I would call around for plane tickets and call her back when I find some.

I then walked outside to grab my paper. When I opened it there was a rose inside. I had the biggest smile on my face; I didn't know what to think. Only Larry loves me with all of his heart and nothing will change that. Not even Lynn will get in the way. I will let her know, not in a mean way, but in a way that she will never forgive Larry again. I will tell her that we love each other and he kissed me. He kissed me in such a way that the sun came up when he did it. I will tell her that she has been selfish and only thinks of herself. I will tell her that something has gotten in the way of fulfilling her dreams and she should move on—move on or even to move away.

Darkness

The sweet silence of the dark
The shining moon so far away
Anguished in the time of death

The ambiguous stars
Moving with freedom
Arranged in sweet sorrow

The time of the Comet
The time of a new beginning
With one flower

She will move or I will make her.

Just then I realized that I was talking crazy and demented. I can't make her go anywhere. I will just explain nicely to her what happened in Italy with Larry and I. Just a romantic kiss, but nothing more than a kiss. We found ourselves having so much fun together and it happened. So Larry has decided to divorce you and be with me. Now all I have to do is find a way to say that to her.

I found some plane tickets on the Internet for cheap. I called Lynn back and told her that I got the tickets. She was very excited about going on a trip with me I told her that we will have a lot of fun and, don't forget, to bring a swimsuit. You never know what the weather will be like.

Chapter Five

A month has passed and we were on our way to San Francisco. I had brought a book to read on the plane. I didn't want to have to talk to her the whole time. I was kind of scared of what might happen when I do tell her. I thought I would pick a place in public so she could not do anything drastic to me.

I was thinking about Larry and how he had put a rose in my paper every morning up until today. I thought about how much he loves me and always will. When we arrived, we waited for our bags and then headed on to our Bed and Breakfast. We settled in and headed down to Fisherman's Wharf. We saw the seals while we were walking on the pier. I knew it would be time for me to tell her soon. She then said she wanted to go see Alcatraz Island. We hopped on the ferry and went over. I then thought to myself that Alcatraz would be a great place to tell her.

I didn't really know we would be wearing headphones. She was so engrossed in the tour that I didn't want to say anything. I began to get into the tour, also, and found myself buying all sorts of junk from the place. I was having so much fun, that I completely forgot to talk to her about the problem. I also had never been to San Francisco, so I wanted to enjoy every minute there.

We went to Coit Tower and the panoramic view was beautiful. I fell in love with it; the lights in the dark *made* the view for me. We decided to go out to eat and found this quaint little Italian restaurant. We ordered a bottle of wine and oysters. I never ate oysters before; they kind of tasted like rubber to me. The wine dulled the taste a lot. I felt like I was drinking like a fish. Lynn then asked me why I was so quiet and distant. I began to tell her, but something stopped me from saying anything. So I asked her how Larry and she were doing. She hadn't really talked about him at all.

"So, how are you two doing these days," I had asked.

"Fine, but I always feel that something is bothering him."

"Do you have a clue at all what might be going on?"

"No, he doesn't talk to me or even touch me anymore."

I did try not to smile, but deep down I was smiling. That made my night, so I wanted to hear more of their problems.

"Oh, I am deeply sorry about that. Did you even try to talk to him about what was bothering you before?"

"No; that night he never came home. He called me that night and said that he was going to stay with Nick at his house so they can work on some figures for the business. I told him that it was fine with me," Lynn said.

"You trust him that much to not even come home?"

"No, but I don't really have a choice. Whatever he says goes and I guess that is fine with me."

"I wouldn't tolerate that."

"If he would have fouled around on me, he would have done it by now."

"Do you even care?" I said.

"No, I don't. I kissed a guy because I thought he was fooling around on me, and a while back there was this girl that called every week and wanted to talk to him. I didn't know what to tell her other than stop calling here."

"Did you confront him on this," I had asked.

"No, I guess I just wanted to fix our marriage and forget everything that has happened in our life. And if he ever screwed around on me I would have him killed. The guy I had kissed is a hit man."

"You know you're scaring me with all of that talk. Where did you ever find a hit man and why would you want to go to jail for something like that."

I didn't really know if I should say anything to her. She was acting kind of weird; maybe all this stuff that has happened in her marriage is damaging her brain.

"So, you find any love yet?" she had asked me.

"No, not yet, but Sam came into town and we had a good time together," I said.

"Anyone else on your list of men in your life?"

"You never answered my question about the hit man."

"I saw him in the bar, he was tall and handsome. I was crying at a table one night and he walked up to me and asked if he could help me with anything. I asked him to kill my husband. We talked for a while and he told me that he would kill anyone for such a beautiful women as myself. So I kissed him on the cheek.

"I thought you kissed a guy for real. Don't scare me like that, I thought he really was a hit man."

"No, but he would kill for me," Lynn said.

"Do you really want that?"

"No, but sometimes people have to be scared for their life."

"Who are you trying to scare, me?"

"Yes. Nick told me that you two hang around a lot at the restaurant."

"We never told you because we didn't want to hurt your feelings."

"I was so happy when you asked me to come here. I wanted to talk to you about him and ask you if he was screwing around on me," she inquired.

I didn't know how to tell her, but this would be the time, the best time of all.

What we are given everyday is in front of us, whether shameful or hurtful. What we decide to do everyday is in front of us. We decide our future, in how we feel or react, and in every situation involving society, in everything which we have to buy or give. People judge you for what you have and do in your life. You have to go for your dream no matter what is in your way.

She had asked me, "So, what is *your* dream and what *are* you trying to say to me. You're trying to tell me that he has fooled around on me. He loves someone else, I just know it."

She started balling her head off; I didn't know what to say to her. Other then let's pay for our meal and get ourselves out of this restaurant. I didn't want to make a scene in that place. She wouldn't stop crying I didn't really want to tell her there was no one. She had her head on my shoulder, just sobbing. I couldn't console her for the life of me. I tried to tell her that maybe he has a good reason for doing that.

She had asked me if I knew who she was.

I told her, "Yes. We went to High School together."

She asked me if she was good looking, and I told her, "Of course. She is very beautiful."

"Do you know her name, or where she lives?"

"I think I am supposed to leave that part up to your husband." I told her that her husband has told me that he loves you and Teddy very much, but this new person brought love to his life.

She wouldn't stop crying. Nothing I would say helped her. I asked if she wanted to go home. She then calmed down enough to tell me that she wants to stay and have fun with me, the best friend she has ever had.

I began to cry then, and she didn't know the real reason, and only thought that I was feeling her pain. I was really crying about me, doing this to a friend that I have had since we were little tots.

The next day we had gone to the Exploratorium and saw the entire wonderful science project. It was really amazing how someone can put together something so beautiful. The mechanics and structure of it all was beyond words. We had gone shopping and spent a load of money.

Lynn drank like a fish the whole day. I didn't really feel that bad about what I was doing last night. By the end of the night I had to drag her back to the Bed and Breakfast where we were staying. I plopped her onto the bed and went to the nearest phone outside the building and called Larry.

He asked me, "So did you get a chance to tell Lynn about us."

"Not exactly. I told her that you were with someone, though."

"What! I wanted you to tell her about the two of us. Then she wouldn't get so upset."

"No matter who you ended up with, she would be just as mad. After I told her the beginning of my speech, she just guessed the end of it. And I wasn't in it; she got very upset and asked me all sorts of questions. I just couldn't. I wanted to, but I told her to ask you when she got home. She drank all day today, so now she is passed out on the bed. That is why I'm calling you right now."

"Well, I guess I can tell her the rest," Larry said.

"Yes, it might be better if it came out of your mouth rather than mine."

"I will talk to you later. Take care."

I had told him likewise, and to begin writing out how

he was going to explain it to Lynn when she got home.

When Lynn woke up in the morning she wanted to go home so she could talk to Larry in person. I called the airport and made our flight sooner. We took off at three in the afternoon. We got home around eleven o'clock that night.

She had asked me if I would go into the house with her when she confronts Larry, but I had told her 'no way.' That is something they will have to work out themselves.

The flight home was quiet and I wrote a poem about our trip. Even though I have feelings for her husband, I still considered her my friend, even though she might not think so after she finds out about Larry and I kissing and going to Italy together.

New Friends

As the mountains are high
The ocean is low

How curious the birds
So swell I suppose

As you see Coit Tower
From everywhere you go

One step here and one step there

The hills are high
The hills are there

As we may walk or drive we see

Shops and cuisine
Too tempting to leave

As we may end our night one day
We taste something new, so exciting I say

The morning is chilly
The fog could be there

As we see so many buildings
So beautiful standing there

The line and structure so fine, there left to be
The place of Fine Arts, is the one to see

Soon we find our bodies standing in the ocean
We have one thought, cold is the motion

As we see the mountains, amber they are
The feeling of freedom enter my mind

As I finished with the poem we were landing on the ground. I was amazed at how fast everything went. Lynn had given me a hug and took a taxi home. I had given her my best wishes and my love, and hoped the best for her.

That night I went home and wrote another poem.

There's more to life then two cups of coffee

To see and hear
Adds complications and fears

To smile adds a great happiness
That lasts for a long while

To feel more than one
Adds something inside that makes it real

Right now I would not want to be Larry. He has a lot coming home to him. I would love for him to come to my house tonight and say he was kicked out. It was now one o'clock in the morning and I haven't heard from him yet, so I went to bed.

A long day comes to an end for me.

Chapter Six

The next morning I woke up and Larry was sleeping on my porch. I rushed out to get him and wake him up. He looked like a ball just curled up so cute. I shook him to wake him up. He woke up and I asked him what happened last night, and if he told her about us. Now he really didn't have a great look on his face.

"Yes, I told her about us; but she didn't believe me."

"What? Why wouldn't she believe you? Is she insane? You flat out told her and she didn't believe you?"

"Yes. How many times do I have to tell you? She didn't believe it was you. She knows it is someone, but she thinks I said your name to cover it up."

"So, she's not mad at the fact that it was us. It's crazy to think of it that way. So, now what are we going to do?"

"She told me to get out so she could think about what has happened and to come back tomorrow and we could talk some more. I will go back there today and talk to her."

We sat there at my kitchen table and talked about what we are going to do and how he should talk to her about things that happened. A couple hours had passed and then he left to go back to his house.

Jack came into my room to ask me some questions about what I have been writing. I didn't know what to tell him. I began to tell him that I am to the point of frustration; that I am not sure why she didn't believe him. The fact is, I love this guy more than anyone does, and I am scared to find out what happens next. The way I feel when I write this, is, frankly, awful.

I feel that something is going to go wrong. I don't

want to write any more; I am scared to know. What if he dies or what if she dies? I feel as though if something happens to him, I won't be able to survive this and will die. Jack told me that I am alive right now and I shouldn't be that worried. What's important right now, is to figure out why you are here and what brought you here. He told me that he wants me to continue writing. Then Jack told me that he had written a poem to cheer me up and to know that something good will come of this, and not to worry about anything that has happened.

Travels

The sight of the beyond
So original and full of Passion

Things we found boundless
Full of artistic harmony

Everywhere you looked
Brought to you, exude cheerfulness

When he came back to my house he had his bags with him. I actually had a smile on my face. He walked up to my door and said, "Honey, I'm home."
 I ran to him and gave him a big hug and kiss. I was happy that he came.
 I asked him, "So, what did she say?"
 He told me she thought about what had happened and she was very mad. She had thought about what I had said to her in San Francisco and I should remember what she had told me. He didn't quite get what she was talking

about.

He then asked, "What did she mean by that? Was there something that she had done?"

"Well, when we were talking about some things she told me that she had kissed someone."

"What in the world are you talking about? When would she even have the chance?"

"I suppose it was when we were in Italy, she told me you had gotten various phone calls from a girl and she told me that she just told her to stop calling. Then she said that she was so mad, she went and got a drink from the bar and kissed a man who said he would kill for her."

"Does that mean that she is going to have me killed?"

"I am not really sure about that. I wouldn't believe that she would be capable of that."

He then told me that he was never with another woman. I told him that he could tell me if he really did and I wouldn't really care at all. He didn't want to talk about this any more. He told me that they did split up forever and they are going to get a divorce.

She couldn't handle all of this wrongful treatment. I told him that I was happy that she kicked him out and now we could be together without sneaking around anymore. He then walked over to me and lifted me up into his arms, gave me a big squeeze and started to walk up the stairs into my bedroom. We got to my bed, he then threw me on it, and I guess you could take it from there.

The next morning I woke up and he was gone already. I went outside and the rose was in the paper again. I thought to myself, if he keeps this up I am going to want to marry that guy. As I was drinking my coffee and reading my newspaper the phone rang. When I answered the phone it was Lynn. She started yelling at me furiously about Italy and how could I do something like that to her. I was supposed to be her best friend and be with her forever.

She said that she was more hurt because it was I, rather than someone else. I had told her what Larry said, that it sounded as if she was okay with all of this. She told me that she was still getting a divorce and she never wanted to talk to me again. It was very wrong that this happened the way it did and she will never forgive me. She said to have a nice life with Larry and remember what she told me.

I really didn't think that she would want to risk her whole life on killing someone. Plus, she would never see Teddy ever again. I called the restaurant and Nick answered. I asked him if Larry was there, because I had to talk to him. He told me that Larry left town for a couple of days so he could think about what happened.

I told myself that it would have been nice for him to at least tell me when he was leaving, but considering the circumstances of what had just happened, he has a right. I got ready for work and went on my way. When I walked in, there was a dozen roses sitting on my desk, with a note attached saying which said, "I went to go see my lawyer. I will be back in a couple of hours. Just trying to keep you on your toes. Love and Always, Larry."

What a sweet guy and he sure does love the roses. I called Sally today and talked to her on the phone about all of this. She said that Lynn was just upset and that's why she's talking all crazy and everything. She just lost someone that she's been with for six years. They have a son together and I think she's just worried about what's going to happen to her financial situation.

I thought to myself, that she wasn't very good at keeping that in order. I thought back on the entire time we spent together, dreaming about whom we would be with, what he would look and act like. Would he be smart and pretty or dumb and handsome? We would like to have a little of both—that's what we both have always wanted.

Sally told me that we had done right. There would be no other way for us to be together, if we hadn't said anything to her. I got back to work and I couldn't stop thinking of what's been going on. I gave Chris a call, to come in to work for me the rest of the day. He told me that he would, after I told him what had been going on. He lives pretty close to here, so it didn't take him long to come here. I grabbed my roses and went home. When I got there, I went upstairs to go to bed.

Later that night Larry had come home. We ended up talking all night, about what his lawyer had said to him. His lawyer had told him that it was good that we were so honest and caring about her feelings. He would have to pay child support and he would have Teddy every weekend and summers. About his household items and property, they would have to split everything fifty-fifty, between both of them. He probably will be able to keep the business if they negotiate enough. It was so wonderful to hear that, and hoping it goes okay. His lawyer also said that it will only go that smoothly if Lynn's lawyer is nice. Lynn is the victim and she will have a little more leverage over all of this.

Larry then told me that he had to work the next couple of days, but then he had taken another week off. Nick understands and he really doesn't have anything else to do. After our long exhausting night of conversation, we went to bed. While we were lying there in bed, I thanked him so much for the roses. He told me it's for being there for him through all of this. Then I told him thanks for the roses in the paper every morning. He gave me a questionable look and said that he wasn't the one doing that. I didn't know what to think. I was very puzzled about this whole thing.

Chapter Seven

The next morning I called the paper and asked them who the person was who delivered my paper every morning to me. I wanted to know if he was the person who was doing this for me. They gave me *her* name, but not her phone number, but I didn't really think it was a girl giving me the roses. I thought about this, staying up all night to figure out whom it might be. Maybe I might see the person or even get a glimpse.

Larry had to work all day and so he wasn't here in the morning to see him. He didn't even get home until three o'clock in the morning. I couldn't even keep myself awake all night. I ended up falling asleep on my couch and didn't wake up until seven in the morning. Larry was sleeping in my bed and there was a rose in my paper again. This time was different; there was a note-attached reading,

> *For when the time comes*
> *And the moon is glowing*
> *My face will appear*
> *And you will know who I am*

I thought that was so very weird. This person has been admiring me for a while now. Larry woke up a little while later and I told him what had happened. He told me that I don't need to worry about this too much. If this guy were dangerous he would have done something by now. He told me he had to work all day again today, and that we will do something together tomorrow.

I was thinking about this guy and the roses all day. One of the reasons why I fell more in love with Larry is because of the roses with the paper. So original that I thought this was a sign for me to go through with this. It was the kiss first for me, and then the roses told me to go through with it.

But now, I didn't know what to think. Who was doing this and why wouldn't he show his face. What was he waiting for? Larry has been so nice to me and we fell in love. But this rose thing is bugging me; I want to know who is doing this. I thought to myself that I needed a hot bath. So I decided to take a bath and write some more.

Hidden

> For something you couldn't see
> For something you couldn't hear
>
> Like a ringing of a bee
> That makes you run in fear
>
>
> For something you couldn't find
> For something you couldn't leave
>
> Like something missing behind
> That makes you want to believe
>
>
> For something you could feel
> For something you could love
>
> Like something that heals
> And makes two flying doves

It really bugs me; I started to think about what this guy might look like and why he is stalking me. I decided to take a walk around the neighborhood and try to see if there was someone who might be doing this. Maybe he lives around here and is just trying to scare people.

It was a very nice day to have a walk; a little cool, but nice. As I was walking along the sidewalk, the trees were swaying in the wind. There were people mowing their lawn and raking their leaves. There was an older guy who I always see outside on my way to work, just standing on his porch. I had said 'hi' to him. He came up to me and said, "Aren't you the women that lives a block down from here?"

"Yes, my name is Jane. Sorry we haven't met before. I always try to get out and greet my neighbors, but my job doesn't really let me."

"Well, what do you do?"

"I own a clothing store in town."

"Well, it's always nice to see my neighbors."

He started to walk back to his house and I shouted out,

"Hey, have you seen anything unusual lately going on around here."

He then turned around and said, "Like what?"

"Well, for a few months now there has been this person who leaves roses in my paper every morning and I was just wondering if you have seen anyone that just moved in or just some one new walking around here."

"No, nothing unusual around here."

He then turned around and went back on his porch. I thanked him for his help, and went on. I thought to myself that I haven't seen anyone move in to any of the houses or any houses for sale.

I haven't been on a walk for a long time, either. I thought to myself, getting a dog would be kind of fun. I have always wanted a lab, but a beagle would be fun to have. It's easier to take care of, and it's a smaller dog. Well, I started to walk back home and this guy came out of nowhere. He was a cute one. He was walking his Springer towards me. As we passed, we smiled and said 'hi' to each other.

I had said to him, "Nice day outside; a great day to walk your dog."

He said, "Yes, it is," and kept on walking.

I haven't seen his face around here; maybe he's the one. He was tall, cute, but not very talkative.

When I got back home there was a message on my answering machine. It was from Lynn wanting to talk to Larry about the divorce. She wanted to get together tomorrow and have lunch and decide what they were going to do. She told him to bring his lawyer.

I didn't know what to think, it was all a big mess. And all of this happened because of me. I guess Larry had a big part in it to. I was actually with someone that loved me. He's getting a divorce for me; it seemed like he would do anything for me. I lost a friend but I had gotten a lover. A great one, in fact—strong, dependable, and a very nice guy, who always has something to say, and always has a come-back for everything.

When Jack and I got together, he said that I was progressing very well. He was wondering what I thought about this person that had put the roses in my paper every morning. I told him that it just confused me more than anything. I loved the fact that it was a mystery, and I have to figure out who's doing this, but it scares me. I guess I love this Larry and I want to spend the rest of my life with him, but at this moment I was trying to understand why.

Why was this guy doing this to me and what did he want from me? Why did he start now? Where is he living and where is he from? I feel that everything at this moment is very confusing, but a little exciting, too. Jack said for me to keep writing—he wanted to know everything…how I felt, how Larry and I were doing. I feel he is really getting into my life and really wants to help me remember more and more.

I didn't even want to stay up last night so I just went to bed. Again Larry had gotten home at three a.m. in the morning and there was a rose, but no note. I wondered why this was, or if he is just doing this to make me wonder even more, to keep me guessing as to what he is going to do next.

As I sat they're drinking my coffee and reading my paper. I came across an article about how this guy saved his wife from a burning building out of town. As I read the article I noticed that he loved his wife very much and would risk his own to save his wife. They have been married for twenty years and wanted no one else in their lives.

At the end of the article it read, "I love you, Sam, with all my heart and I hope you will stay with me for the rest of my life." And the words love-will-stay was underlined in the sentence. My first reaction was that this mystery guy had done this and then I wondered what he meant. I then quickly looked through the rest of the paper to find out if he underlined any other words.

Just as I was doing that Larry had walked downstairs and asked me, "What are you doing? You're going through that paper like you're a mad-women on drugs."

"Oh, I was just trying to find out where the weather section was."

I didn't want him to know that I was obsessing over this rose thing. He did mention that I had gotten another rose again and was wondering if he had written a note, also. I told him that there wasn't a note this time. Then I tried to change the subject and told him that Lynn called yesterday and wanted him to get together today and have lunch.

She also said to bring your lawyer because she would like to discuss the divorce. Larry said, of course, she would. Well, at least he has the day off to do so. He also mentioned how he missed Teddy and not being able to see him every day.

When he called Lynn to make the arrangements, I got ready to go to work for a couple of hours to do paperwork. I wished him good luck and had gotten a great kiss out of it. I then quickly grabbed the paper and ran out the door. He didn't see me take it and, wow, what a nice kiss! I was surprised that he would be able to give me such a kiss through all of what is going on.

When I got to work, I just had to look at the paper. My anticipation to know was driving me crazy. I am surprised that I didn't look at the paper while I was driving. I was just crazy, insane to think that he would have time to underline a whole bunch of words. As I was looking through the paper, nothing else was underlined.

I was surprised that he didn't do anything else but those three words, love-will-stay. What did that mean? I thought I couldn't wait until he showed me more. I just have to keep this away from Larry, just so he doesn't think that I am going overboard with this whole thing. I went through the paper and rushed out of there.

Sally asked me how everything is going and I said great. She asked me if we were going to have our meeting tonight and I said that it would have to wait a couple more weeks. I am really busy and right now with everything going on, we possibly can't do it right now. I told her she was doing a great job and there should be a raise in her future.

I rushed out of there to go home and see how Larry's visit with Lynn went. When I got home I wondered why he wasn't there yet. I wondered if something happened to him. Lynn had told me before that she would have him killed. I was scared, but I don't think she is capable of doing such a thing.

The stress of thinking too much got to me. I went into the refrigerator and grabbed a beer. I wanted to relax and wait for him. I walked out on the porch, grabbed my pen, a paper, and started to write. I just wrote whatever was on my mind.

Colors

As the wind blows
The leaves crackle

Fall is here

Cool nights are upon us
As the yellow leaf says

Why must we leave?
Asked mister red

BEAUTIFUL!
BEAUTIFUL!

As nature becomes us
We tend to color the land

To make one night
Feel like an incredible strand!!!

It is so beautiful outside. When the leaves are changing colors you feel different, like something is going to happen to you. I look outside at all the maple trees and their colorful leaves. It's so incredible that I wish the trees could always stay that beautiful. Kind of like us, at one time we all look beautiful. And then we change, too. Time changes and we go with it.

Larry finally showed up and I asked him how everything went, and why it took so long. He walked right past me and didn't say anything. I didn't know whether he was mad or he was just in his own world. I walked in right after him and asked him if he was okay, and if he needed anything. When he started to talk his words came out all wrong. He was drunk, he told me that Lynn upset him and the whole damn meeting upset him. I said, well, then, we could talk in the morning. He ended up passing out on the couch and I just went to bed. I guess no sleeping on the couch for me tonight.

That night I couldn't sleep. I tried to, but this rose man was getting to me. I wanted to know who it was so badly that I ended up staying awake all night and he never came. It was like a bad dream. When the paper came there was no rose. I wondered why he wouldn't put a rose in this morning paper and he did in all the rest of them.

When Larry woke up he was still so drunk that he didn't even want to talk to me. I asked him if everything went all right, he didn't say anything. He walked in to the bathroom and took a shower. After he came out, he told me that she is going to take him for everything he has. He began to say that maybe this divorce wouldn't be worth all of this trouble.

Then he said that I am worth everything to him, but he doesn't want to deal with all of this. If she takes everything from him he will be devastated. His business is everything to him and without that I am not sure if he would continue his life as a normal guy.

I fell in love with him and it will hurt me if he is hurting inside. I didn't know what to say to him. I began to think that maybe, just maybe, I will tell him to not get a divorce. That might not be what he wants. What if he goes berserk and flies off the handle. Oh, I really don't know.

I ended up saying to him, "Maybe you should just wait until you talk to your lawyer; he might have some ways of going around it."

"I know that I am going insane over all of this and I shouldn't be. You're right, I will wait. What would I do with out you? You're a lifesaver. Thanks, Jane, it's nice to know that you really care about me."

"Well, of course I do, I care a lot about you. I don't want anything to happen to you. But, just take it slowly, I am in no rush."

We then talked about what we were going to do tonight. He thought that we could have Chinese food and a movie. I told him that it sounded great, but what sounded better is maybe we should order in and cuddle up in front of the TV. We decided to spend the night relaxing. He went to go get the Chinese food and a movie. I spent that time setting up the house. I changed the living room around, so that the couch faced the TV with the chairs on either side.

I lit all the candles in the house and set the kitchen table. I ended up using the rose pedals to scatter on the table, kind of an Italian remembrance thing. I did the same thing to the coffee table and scattered candles on it, too. I just thought it would take his mind off things a little bit and also mine.

I just can't get that stupid rose man out of my head. I know that being together tonight will make it all go away. I thought it was taking him a long time to get the stuff. I got dressed into something comfy and sat on the couch to wait for him. I thought writing would waste some time right now.

Lost

As his arm just barely touches me
It sends shivers threw my body

As our eyes meet each other's
It feels like I am in Heaven

His words sound like poetry

As his cologne fills the room
It smells as though you could eat him

When he wraps his arms around me
I never want him to let go

I feel as though I am lost
And will never be found again

Then he whispers in my ear
And gives me a smile

I feel as though there's hope
And he will be here soon

Love is one thing. It's just like me, I obsess over everything, like Larry and now the rose man. When I think of Larry and how good he makes me feel it drives me nuts to the bones. The way his lips move across my neck. The way his hands massage my body. His soft and gentle touch. Just the way he kisses me, it's as if he sends me to another dimension.

My body falls faint; my legs feel like rubber. It feels so good to be loved and to show it. But now I think of this rose man. What he looks like, and why he is doing this? But I don't want Larry to know that this is going on with me.

Larry finally showed up and I asked him why he was gone so long. He explained to me that there was a long line at the Chinese place. He also couldn't decide what movie to get. I told him whatever movie he picks I am sure it will be fine. I trust his judgment; it's fine.

As he was looking around the place, he thought it looked really cool. That made me so happy inside. The night was so romantic and relaxing. We didn't talk about the divorce at all. I thought that it was nice of him to not say anything.

As we watched the movie his fingers were gently

rubbing my arms. As the candles were flickering, I felt like my body was falling. I felt so relaxed that it scared me. Then he took off his shirt, Oh! He was to die for. His soft muscular chest was so sexy. As he slid down on the couch and put his legs on the coffee table I lay my head on his chest. He put his hand on my head and held me tightly.

I was in heaven that night. We ended up falling asleep on the couch. When I woke up, I ran outside to check to see if the paper was there. There was a rose this morning, I felt so excited about it. When I opened the paper up a note fell out. I didn't want to read it; I pulled it close to my chest and peeked over to the couch to see if Larry was still sleeping. I carefully opened the note and it read.

When the leaves blow
And the dogs bark
We will shake hands

Oh! My! This guy is crazy. I think he is driving me insane. At that moment Larry woke up, I quickly put the note in my pocket and said, "Good morning, how do you like your eggs. I thought I would cook you breakfast before I have to go to work and you have to go to the lawyer."

"That sounds wonderful, how about over-easy?"

"I could do that for you, why don't you hop in the shower and breakfast will be ready for you when you get out."

We enjoyed our breakfast together and went our ways.

When I got to work I just had to call someone about this. I got hold of Sally and she said 'what is that supposed to mean?' I didn't really know, either. She told me to call the cops and have this checked out.

"Maybe he is leaving prints on the papers or the roses. Maybe you could put cameras out on your porch just to find out who is doing this. Or, just maybe, it is Larry doing this and he is just trying to see how you react."

"It couldn't be Larry doing this. We slept on the couch together and we didn't move."

"He could have drugged you and you didn't even feel him moving during the night. Then he went back into place and faked sleeping in the night."

"Sally, you have been watching too many movies in your lifetime. He just couldn't possibly be doing this. I will see you later, when you get here."

We hung up and I got back to work.

Later that night Larry had gotten home and we discussed this whole thing again. He told me not to worry about it. He hasn't done anything yet, so we'll just wait and see what happens. That right there makes me believe that he is doing these things. I guess I am going to wait. You never know what might happen, but it makes my life a bit more exciting around here.

Chapter Eight

A couple months have past and Larry is still living with me. I am still getting the roses and I am not sure who it is, yet. The weird thing is that now I am getting them every other day and not every day.

Larry got a quickie divorce and is very happy about it. Lynn came to her senses and let Larry have Teddy every weekend and summers. He has to pay child support and he had to give Lynn the car. He kept the business and loves it right now. He does leave a lot to go on business trips some weeks. But that really doesn't bother me. We spend all the rest of the time together. It's not as if he leaves every week; it's just about once a month and only for a couple of days.

This last time he went he brought home a gift for me. I collect antiques and he finds the best ones for me. I got a box, but not just an ordinary box. It was an old milk crate; I put all of my dried roses in it. I kept everyone of them, to remind me, that I haven't gotten this figured out, yet.

Someday, I know I will. I had finished with work for the day and I stopped by the bar. Larry was out of town and I didn't feel like going home yet. Now that he was living with me it isn't scary to be home alone. I don't know how I would be totally alone, especially when this guy is still stalking me.

Lynn still isn't talking to me, at least, not to my face. She say's 'hi' on the phone when she calls for Larry, but that's about it. No mean words, or even 'nice weather out there' or 'how are you doing?' just natural things like that. Not that I expect her to be nice to me. It's just that we have been friends for a lifetime. I miss having our chat's together. I want her to start, or maybe she wants me to start.

Jack just came into my room. He wanted to know why it was taking me so long to figure out why I am still here.

I said, "Well, Jack, I am just enjoying our time that we spend together."

"Smart ass!"

"No, really! I have been having a lot of fun. It's like I am writing my journal all over again."

"Well, at least someone is having fun," Jack said.

"Are you distressed about something?" I asked him.

"We just got a new person in here today. He's really angry and disturbed about something. I didn't want him here, but they sent him anyway. I can't tell you anymore of it."

"I hope you keep that guy locked in one of those special rooms. The people that come in here sometimes really freak me out."

"Don't worry, you will never have to see him, unless he gets better in a hurry."

"You know, I was really wondering about my business and my home. Now that I know that I have had those, I would like to know if they're still mine or if they had to sell them, or if someone I knew owns them right now."

Jack told me, "I am not able to tell you any details of your life, in fear it will damage your healing process."

"That's a bunch a crock," I yelled at him.

He turned his back and said, "Get back to your writing and then maybe I will let you outside to do your gardening."

Jack sounded very disturbed, as if something had just hit him over the head and he is really pissed about it.

I am wondering about my business, home and everything else I had in my life at one time. Wondering if they are still around or if something strange happened. The last couple of days I have been drawing on my wall with my pen. I know I will probably get in trouble, but who cares! It's something fun to do right now. It's a picture of the weeping willow outside my window. That's all the further I have gotten, I was thinking of adding the garden or even Mr. Jack. That would really piss him off, although I would have to do that last. Otherwise I believe he would probably get mad at me.

That night, before I went to bed, I wanted to watch a movie. I was flipping through the channels and thought I had seen something out of the corner of my eye. I looked over and there was no one there. I was a little scared, but Larry was upstairs sleeping!

I guess I shouldn't be scared about it, but I am. This guy was stalking me and I still don't know why. I went back to watching my movie. Although I kept on glancing at the window, and even got up a couple of times to look outside, I saw nothing.

Finally I had to shut the window curtains because it really started to scare me. I never saw anything out there. I thought maybe my mind was playing tricks on me or maybe I wanted to see something. This whole thing with this rose guy is giving me the creeps. After that, I grabbed my black and white fuzzy blanket and ran upstairs. I hopped into bed, slid under my covers and cuddled up with Larry. I always feel safe with him, he a great protector. He also is a light sleeper, so I ended up waking him.

He asked me, "Why are you shivering so furiously? Are you cold? Are you getting sick?"

"No, I just thought I saw something outside, but I think it was my imagination!"

"As long as you're okay, that's all that counts, I am here for you when you need me."

That morning I woke up, and no rose. So it was just my imagination, all in my mind. I over-reacted over the whole thing. We both had to work this morning. We said our good-bye's and right before I was to leave the house, Larry grabbed my arms and pulled me closer to him. He told me not to worry about this whole thing with the rose guy. Because he said that *he* is here for me, no matter what happens. I told him that he already said that last night. He wanted to make sure that I knew it, he replied.

It was really important for him to tell me. I knew he cared for me, and that was important for me, too. I waited all my life for this to happen to me—for someone like Larry to be this guy in my life. What happened last night really scared me. I don't know what I will do if this guy really appears.

It's just so weird that he hasn't tried to contact me in a different way. With just those notes and underlining in the paper, I guess maybe this guy might be afraid, too. He hasn't shown his face because he is afraid. Afraid so much that he tries to tell me through his notes and underlinings in the papers.

After I am done with work I thought that I would invite Sally and Chris over to help me try to piece all of it together. I told them everything that has been going on so they would probably be willing to help me. After I called both of them and explained it, they were willing to help me.

It was Saturday, today, so my shop closed at six. I told them to meet me at seven at my house and we could get started on all the extensive work. I had told them it was my treat for the pizza tonight so not to eat anything before they came, and not to make any other plans as we would have a long night ahead of us.

The ticking of the clock began. I was actually getting excited about getting together tonight. I went through some of the items on my desk, just to see if there were any more of the papers or notes that the rose guy had given me.

Today wasn't that busy, but the people that did come in bought a lot of clothes. They had events coming up, like business events and weddings. It was fun, but now I have to close the store for the night.

I grabbed the stuff I needed and raced on home. I had ordered the pizzas from Larry's restaurant and told Larry what we were all doing tonight. I wanted to be totally truthful to him and let him know all of what I was doing.

He said to me, "I guess that really scared you last night, thinking you saw something peering in at you through the window."

I told him that it just gives me the creeps and I want to know what this guy is trying to tell me.

When Sally and Chris got here, I already started to write all of his sayings on paper. I went to the supply store and got a poster-board and I gave Sally the task of gluing the sayings on the board. I told her to glue the ones that I have already written on the paper.

I gave Chris the job of trying to put all of this together in is head. I could put them in order of when I received them; I couldn't remember which came first. So I have randomly written them on the paper,

For when the time comes
And the moon is glowing
My face will appear
And you will know who I am

When the leaves blow
And the dogs bark
We will shake hands

Love-will-stay

I-will-find-a-way

When Two eyes meet
For the first time
My heart will melt

People-die-insane

It's-sunny-out

As I am writing these down on paper I am thinking to myself, this guy doesn't make any sense. It has to be out of order, somehow. Chris and Sally were stumped also. They didn't know what to do. The looks on their faces scared me; it's as if seeing it on paper made it all real to them. They are frightened for me. I told them that Larry keeps on telling me not to be scared about it because he hasn't done anything to me, yet.

"So, he just might be harmless. In fact, maybe he is crazy for me," I told him.

Larry told me, just don't be scared about it, because he is here for me whenever I need him.

Leaves-fall-sadly   *will-end-someday*

Your eyes are beautiful   *door-to-door*
Your hair is long
Your body just sang me a song

Laugh-together-inside   *peace-talks-tomorrow*

Roses-after-roses   *gates-open-slowly*

Flood-fog-storm   *People-will-walk*

Money will fall
Rolled into a ball
Fire destroys all

It's not as if he wrote a saying to me each time, but to try to figure it out was beginning to be impossible. I am not sure if I have gotten all the sayings. Maybe I am missing the most important ones.

Chris said, "We should try to keep going. Now he is sure that this guy is trying to tell us something."

I told him, "Maybe he is just bored and had nothing better to do with his life then to harass me."

Sally said, "I have all night. Let's just go on with this. Let's start putting all the similar words together and maybe that will bring us to a conclusion."

I told her, "Maybe it will bring us to a dead-end. Maybe we are reading into this too deeply and there is nothing to come of it. I am just so very frustrated about all of this, I want it to end."

Chris said, "Let's continue, I really think he's trying to tell us something. Whether or not it's about you or something else, we have an obligation to find out what is going on!"

"Ok, Ok, let's continue this charade!" I said.

We started to put all the like words together and left the sayings for last. We thought just maybe, we would come up with something.

GATES   OPEN   LOVE   WILL   STAY

PEOPLE   WILL   FIND

IT'S   WAY   SUNNY   OUT   INSANE   SADLY

LEAVES   LAUGH   TOGETHER

AFTER   WALK   ROSES   WILL   TALKS

ROSES   WILL   DIE   PEOPLE   END   TALKS

FLOOD   FALL   FOG

SOMEDAY   TO   INSIDE   STORM   I

SLOWLY   DOOR   A   DOOR   PEACE

Then we got rid of the repeated words and figured out a way to make the saying work with the remaining words.

Flood gates will open. After people sadly find it's way to fall inside a storm. Peace talks slowly leaves someday love roses laugh. I stay insane together. Fog walk out, sunny door end.

Well, we kept racking our brains to find another way to say it. After many times of going through and picking the words apart we finally came to the answer that we thought fit the best. We're not sure if it's the right one, or even if it's remotely close, and we haven't figured out how the sayings exactly fit in, either.

> Will people stay together? Find a way to laugh inside, after I sadly walk out insane. Flood gates open, love slowly leaves. Peace talks die. Someday, sunny roses fall. Storm fog, its door end.

I know we have to be missing words. It still doesn't make sense. We think we figured out what he was trying to say, 'His face will appear, when it's dark. He thinks I am good looking.' So we know he has seen me more than once. And he is saying 'money will burn.' I don't understand the 'barking' one and how it fits in.

Maybe he is saying that there are two people in love. They get into a fight and find a way to fix it. Things then get in the way and there is more there that can ever be fixed. So, the fog rolls in and the door shuts tight. Also he knows what I look like and he thinks I am attractive. The others will come in time.

Chris's interpretation of it is that, 'maybe someone had died and he is hurt. Two people were in love with each other and a flood came in and washed his beloved away. He wants that to end. So now he is looking at me.'

I told Chris, I know he has some feelings for me but he doesn't even know me.

Sally said, "Maybe he does. Maybe he has known you for his whole life and has never had the guts to say anything to you."

I told them that they were both insane. If he has known me, he would have brought himself to my attention already. No one could be that shy; besides, he had to have spent a fortune on roses for me. Chris said, "Maybe he grows his own." Sally said that was possible, a lot of people have mini greenhouses in their yards. I told them that maybe I will check those out tomorrow.
"Let's call it a night guys. Thank you so very much for all of your help tonight."
So they both replied, "That means we get a raise."
"Yeah, right—go home and get some sleep. We'll talk later."

That night it kept going through my mind—everything we had talked about and what if we have known each other for years. What if he says 'hi' to me everyday and I don't even know it. I wonder if he's old and creepy, or maybe he is young and cute. Maybe he is trying to give me the creeps intentionally.
That night I suddenly felt sick. I think it was from the stress of trying to figure out what was going on. I thought I would take a long, hot, soothing bath, relax, and think about this whole thing. I ended up falling asleep in the bathtub. I woke up in the middle of the night freezing to death.
When I looked up, Larry was standing above me smiling. I told him that he really startled me; I asked him why he didn't wake me. He really did scare me. He told me that I had a really big surprise waiting for me in the bedroom. He handed me my green robe, I slipped it on.

He told me that he read what we had worked on all night. He said it made sense, in a way. I told him that we had a really hard time trying to figure out what he was trying to say to us, but 'thank you.'

He then covered my eyes with his hand and walked me through my bedroom door. The anticipation was just killing me. He quickly pulled his hand a way and there was a yellow Lab sitting on my bed.

I screamed, "Oh! Thank you. Thank you, so much! It's just what I need right now. It will keep me busy while you're working nights. And Teddy will love it when he comes and stays here."

Larry told me that it made him happy to see a real smile on my face!

I had asked him what was that supposed to mean.

He said that I have been holding my head down for the last couple months, whether or not I noticed it or was trying to ignore it. It hasn't worked. He said that he knows that the rose thing has been bugging me the whole time, and I shouldn't have tried to hide it from him.

He told me that he had gotten the dog from a friend of his and he is already potty trained, and will also be a great protector for me.

Larry said, "With a few lessons, he will be a great watch dog."

I gave him a great big hug and a kiss and thanked him for everything that he has done for me. It is so sweet of him to think of me as much as he does. He told me that I could pick the name for him. I told him I would like to call him 'Bear.'

Chapter Nine

That morning I woke up I did receive a rose, but there was no message with it. I was wondering if he was done writing to me or if he was taking a break from it. This was the second day he hasn't written to me and I was beginning to worry about it. I had decided to go out and look through neighborhood for greenhouses this morning. Larry had to work today; Sundays are a big day for him on business.

I had gotten ready and went to look through the neighborhood. I took Bear with me so I didn't feel so dumb walking around the streets looking to see if anyone has a green house in their yards. We walked for a couple of blocks and I didn't see anything around. I had all day and it was a pretty nice day outside. The sun was shining, beating down at us. Giving us that warmth we love. It feels so good to have the sun out on the very first day I am able to walk my dog, Bear.
He's having a great time, chasing his own shadows on the sidewalk. He is just such a beautiful dog; I am so lucky that Larry gave him to me. Next weekend we start having Teddy at our house and he is going to love Bear. I decided since we have walked six blocks that we will just walk further and go into town. I have to get him a couple of dog treats anyway. In the mean time I was still looking for greenhouses and I still didn't see any around. There was a florist in town so I will go there and ask them about it.

When we got there we went into the florist first and I asked the person at the counter, "Do you know of anyone who has their own greenhouse, or if anyone has bought an abundant amount of roses, lately?"

"No" the florist said. "I don't know of anyone nearby having there own greenhouse. But there was this guy that kept on calling and having roses sent to this girl, sometimes with a note attached though we never knew what it said. We didn't want to open it and have him find out."

"Why? Is he scary, mean or ugly?"

"No, I'm not sure. He always had someone run the note to us. But it always felt like he was watching me, so I never asked any questions about it."

"Well, thanks for your help," I told her.

We went to the pet store and Bear had a lot of fun. I let him pick out his own toy and bone. Larry was right, a pet was all that I needed to make myself feel better. I find myself smiling a lot more. He has done so many funny things today. As we were walking through the pet store I turned the corner really fast and bumped into this guy.

I apologized to him and told him that this was the first walk the dog has had, and I am still trying to train him so he will stop pulling me around. It feels like he is ripping my arm out sometimes.

I then looked down and noticed he had a Springer. I said to him, that I thought I knew him from somewhere. He looked familiar, and then I remembered it was that day I had taken a walk previously.

He then said very quickly that it was nice bumping into me again, but he had to go. He also told me to have the best of luck with my new dog. I had thanked him, paid for my items and headed on home. Bear was behaving a little better when we walked home. Surprisingly enough, I wasn't very mad that I hadn't gotten anywhere on finding out about the greenhouses. I don't know if I wanted it to stay a surprise or if I didn't want to know because I was too scared of finding out what might happen.

When we got home, I lay down on the couch and cleared my mind of everything. I thought to myself that I really needed a vacation of my own; just a getaway from all of what has been going on. I thought to myself that renting a cabin would be a great idea. I would pack the bare essentials and bring Bear with me just to feel safe.

The more I thought about it the more I loved the idea. I could relax and read for a whole weekend and not be bothered with work or even think about the roses all the time. It was enough to give me an ulcer, already.

The other night just thinking about all of that stuff was driving me insane. I picked up a phonebook and called around regarding all the cabins I could find listed. I found one but it was a three-hour drive from here. I thought, well, that actually could be wonderful. I would stop at all the antique stores I could find. I made the plans for next weekend.

When Larry got home I told him that I was going away for the weekend. He thought that would be great for me. He asked me if I was taking Bear with me and I told him of course, I will. I wouldn't keep this guy away from me for a minute. I was crouched down on the floor petting Bear; he just loves that.

I told Larry I would relax, read, and write poetry all weekend. That week went by and I had just remembered that Teddy was coming for the first time. Oh, I felt so bad that I wasn't going to be there when he came, but Larry told me that don't worry about it. It will be good for Teddy and he to spend sometime alone together, especially since it will be his first time here. He told me not to worry about it and go and have fun.

I told him that I always love how supportive he is and understanding of my feelings.

That weekend I went and got the last of the items that I would need. Pop, hot chocolate, graham crackers, Hershey bars, marshmallows, bones for Bear, travel size dishes for him and a few other things. I packed the car up and headed on our way. I popped R.E.M. in the radio and drove on. I waved to Larry as I was leaving the driveway. When I cranked up my radio, he just shook his head and smiled back. He yelled really loudly to, "Have a great time."

I had yelled back, "Don't worry I will."

The drive was so much fun; I had stopped at all the shops on the way and all the rest stops for Bear. I brought my camera to take pictures of him running around. He was having so much fun; he jumped up and tried to drink out of the water fountain. I got a lot of pictures of that. I am so happy I decided to take this trip.

At one of the antique stores I stopped at, I bought these old candlestick holders. I thought they would look great on top of my television, along with the frame I had gotten to match them. It would be great with a picture of Bear in it. At another store I bought these beautiful hand-blown glass bottles.

I was going wild. I thought to myself how many times I really get a chance to go and just do whatever I want. And that was exactly what I was doing. I also thought that Larry is very nice to me. What did I ever do to deserve such a great and wonderful man as he is? I wondered if Lynn and Larry were as great as we are now, or if there was always a quirk about their relationship that they just couldn't work out.

Maybe it is that Larry and I don't see each other that

often and that is why it works out so wonderfully.

When I finally got to the cabin I noticed there weren't very many cars in the lot. I walked up to the office and asked if they had any events going on. The lady told me that there was nothing going on but dinner started at six.

She did mention to me there was a guy playing the piano, in the bar tonight. He knew almost any song you could name by heart and he didn't even know how to read music. I told the sweet lady that I would probably check it out tonight and thanked her for all of her help. I finished paying for my cabin and left.

As Bear and I were walking up the path to our cabin, I noticed that it was very beautiful. Fall was almost over, but you could still see all the wonderful colors of the leaves all over the place.

My cabin was number three, one of the farthest ones out here. But I didn't mind. I wanted the cabin to have a fireplace so I could feel extremely nice and cozy, while I warmed up with a great book and hot cocoa. It was getting close to dinnertime, so I had gotten Bear settled in. I brought his bed and a bone that I bought at the pet store before we left.

I thought to myself, it's good that I have a flashlight with me because I couldn't see anything in front of my face at night. While I was walking down there, I heard music and people laughing. I was excited to see what was there and I was craving appetizers like crazy. No diet this weekend, because this is the weekend I will indulge on everything.

When I walked in, there was a big moose head on the wall. To the right there was a couch and straight ahead there was the restaurant. Right down the middle of it there was a huge tropical fish tank and right beside that there were freshwater fish, such as northern, walleye and other varieties. It was so beautiful to look at; fish have their own harmony in themselves. They live in their own world and have no worries as they swim around. They do get eaten occasionally, though. I am sure that they don't know or worry about it. They swim around as free as they want.

The hostess seated me by the window. By this time the moon was shining off the lake very beautifully. At that very moment I thought about Larry and how I missed him. I have only been a way from him for a couple of hours, but there is a part of me that misses him very much. I just know I won't see him for a whole day.

I ordered stuffed mushrooms in clam sauce, with fried onions and a huge glass of beer. The lady thought I was nuts, but I was famished. Plus, I kept on thinking about my Smores that I had to roast over the fire. When I finished my meal, and I did eat all of it in fact, I walked over to the bar and order a Long Island Iced Tea, grabbed a table and sat down to listen to the music for a while.

There was a man that was sitting at the table next to me. I smiled and he walked right over to me, sat down beside me and asked where I was from. By the smell of his breath I knew he was drunk. We ended up talking for a while, and then he walked me back to my cabin. I was kind of glad that he did, because I was afraid to walk back there all by myself.

I told him to come by tomorrow and maybe we could go for a walk, or go canoeing together. He told me that sounded great; he will come by some time in the afternoon.

When I walked back in, Bear was sound asleep on his bed. When I had taken a couple more steps closer to him, his head quickly rose up and looked to see who it was. I told him it was only me and not to worry. I started the fire and got ready for bed. All the lights were off and only the flicker of the fireplace surrounded the room. I thought it was so cool. I probably stayed awake for hours just thinking of everything that has happened in my life. I was wondering if it will change soon. Then I was just thinking of a poem about Larry and how he makes me feel.

To Love

The sweet soft touch of his fingers
Gently swaying across my body
Giving me feeling of jitters
All through every ounce of me

As my heart beats so rapidly
My arms held on so tightly
As my eyes shut tight so gently
I see stars shining brightly

As everything is flying by
As if I'm floating on air
Feeling of weightlessness is mine
For keeps in my heart till the day I die!!!

I felt very relaxed that night; I was in pure heaven. I felt that a big weight has been lifted off of me. Before I knew it, I finally fell asleep. I don't really remember falling asleep, but I did.

The next morning I felt like going for a run. I had so much energy I didn't know what to do with it. Bear had to go outside anyway, so I threw my coat on over my pj's and headed out.

We ended up walking along the lake. He found a stick and wanted me to throw it around. I was having so much fun, I didn't really think about anything else. We did it for a while and headed back to the cabin. I felt like having some hot chocolate and Smores.

I started up the fire again and got all of my wonderful goodies ready. I felt like a kid again. It was just the dog and I having fun together. In a way that sounded really pathetic, just me being alone and having fun, but that is exactly what more people should do for themselves—have fun, be merry, and enjoy their life to the fullest. I needed to be away at this time in my life. It was really good for my soul.

Jack has been reading my book for a while now and it is scaring me. I am wondering why it is taking him so long. Usually he ends up reading a little and then he talks with me. It's as if he is glued to the book and doesn't know what to say.

I then asked him, "What is taking you so long? Is there something wrong with what I wrote?"

"No, I guess I didn't realize that you had so many feelings for Larry. It sounds like they are real and a great part of you still misses him."

"I guess I do. When I write about Larry I feel safe inside, as if he were my protector. That calms me."

"Well, I guess I just wanted you to go back to your room and write about the rest of what happened to you while you were at the cabins.

I started feeding Bear some of the Smores that he liked to eat and we just sat back and listened to the crackling of the fireplace. I loved it as I sat there in the chair facing the fireplace. I felt like I was sinking into it. I was wrapped in my blanket that I brought from home which made it all the better. At that very moment there was a very loud knock at the door. I felt like I jumped about fifty feet in the air.

I said, "Who is it."

He replied, "It's the guy you talked with at the bar last night."

"Oh, I'm sorry. I guess I was in my own little world. I just forgot. I was having Smores, would you like some."

"Well aren't you just the best little campfire girl."

"No, not really. I just felt like pigging-out this whole weekend."

"Did you get dumped? You never did say why you were here."

"I guess I have had so much on my mind that I needed to get away from town. Well, I am ready for that walk now. Do you mind if my dog tags along with us."

"No, not at all, I would love that. I love dogs. Had a lot of them while I was growing up."

We walked and canoed and then walked again for hours. I felt like I knew his whole life story. We decided to go and get a drink in the bar, so I could warm up. We had brought Bear back to my cabin for him to warm up.

I ended up thinking about this guy just as we were in the middle of a conversation. We had a lot in common with each other. I thought it was weird that I could talk to a stranger better then I could ever talk to Larry. There are just some things I can't tell him and which I told this guy.

Just then he asked me if I was okay. I told him I just was thinking of Larry and what he might be doing right now.

He asked, "Why? Don't you trust him right now?"

"Of course I do, it's just that he has his son there for the first time and I was wondering what they were doing. But there is a little of me that thinks he is fooling around on me."

"What gives you that idea, has anyone ever said anything to you."

"His ex-wife was always saying that he was. And he did with me, when he was with her."

"Does he love you?"

"What does that have to do with anything?"

"Does he love you?" he asked me again.

"Well, I thought that he loved his wife and he cheated on her."

"Don't worry. For all that you have told me, he is not cheating on you."

"It's nice to get a man's point of view on it. It makes me feel a little better about Larry and I being together. Although, I guess I really won't know that answer for certain."

The whole time I didn't mention anything about the rose man and what I have been going through with that. I really didn't want anyone else to know about it. This fellow has been a great person to talk to about all of this and it made me feel better knowing more, through is perspective, about some of the things that were going on in my life.

We ended up eating dinner and talking some more about life and the beautiful scenery. I told him I would probably come up here more often, but the fall is just the best time to spend in the woods, especially everything about the leaves and just how they crunch while you walk on them, the beautiful colors of fall, and the crisp smells in the morning.

You know winter is coming, but it still smells as if spring is coming. You hear the birds chirping far away and the streams running down to the river. I guess I love fall more than any other season. The weird thing about fall is that it always makes me think of family and how wonderful it would be to have kids of my own. My age is getting up there and it is about time I started.

I guess Bear can be the start of having kids in my life. Plus, I love dogs, they are so innocent and lovable. It was getting late and I needed to get back to let Bear out. This fellow walked me back and said that maybe we will see each other again soon. I told him it was fun and I hope to see him next fall—same time, same place. As he was walking away, I waved and walked back inside. I had gotten the fire started and let Bear outside to relieve himself.

Later that night, while I was enjoying my book I heard some noise outside. A stick then just broke, and the crunching of the leaves. I remembered that Bear was still outside and right when I began to let him in I glanced back at the window nearest to the fireplace. I saw a silhouette of a person in the window.

I then quickly got Bear inside and held on to him. I was sitting in the middle of the room scared out of my mind. My heart started to race and I began to tremble. I kept on looking out each dark and empty window, as I didn't dare move an inch. I didn't know what to expect and I didn't want anything to happen.

I then saw a shadow on my wall. My eyes grew bigger and I just froze there. My mouth began to get dry and I didn't know what to do. Then one arm began to rise and he had something in his hand. Oh, my! I didn't know what to say. I wanted to scream at the top of my lungs. I thought someone was here to kill me.

Just then the shadow was holding a rose, I was scared, but I then grabbed Bear by his collar and ran to the window. I tried to look out and see who it was, but it was too dark outside.

I then thought about Larry. He is the only one besides Sally and Chris that knows that I am here. How could this man possibly know where I am unless he followed me here? He could be the guy that I was talking with. I have never actually seen him, or if I did, I didn't even know it.

I then walked over to my bed and plopped down on it. I held my head in my hands and started to cry. 'Why me? Why me? Oh, dear God, why me?'

I felt trapped. I knew then that I had to stop being a chicken about this and face my fears. I walked outside and looked to see if there was anything around that the guy might have left. There was a rose at the doorstep wrapped in paper. I brought it inside and began to open it up, after I looked at all the sides. When I opened the paper up there was a note-attached which read,

I will find you
Up the tree
Down the tree
I will find you

So, now I knew that I can't hide from him, and no matter where I go he will find me. I don't like the idea of having a stalker; I know as soon as I get back I will be calling the police about this. I don't care if they think that I am crazy, I want them to watch my house and investigate this whole thing.

I couldn't sleep that night so I wrote a poem to pass the time. As soon as I see the sun I am taking my stuff along with Bear and I will be heading home.

Running Scared

As the shadow surrounds me

Frightened with anticipation

I'm not sure where to reach

As I blink with discretion

The face just disappears

Where did it vanish?

You look behind you

In fear it will appear

You look in front of you

Scared out of your mind

It's gone, nowhere to be found

The fear eats you alive

And just makes you run.

After I wrote it, I left. I packed my bags and we left. I couldn't stand it anymore. I needed to go and get back to Larry. At that moment I wished I had a cell phone.

Chapter Ten

I was unbelievably scared out of my mind. I had to be speeding because I don't really remember how I got home. Before I knew it, I was running up the stairs as fast as I could to get to Larry. I jumped into bed and he freaked.

"What the hell are you doing here?" he said to me.

"I saw him, I saw him."

"You saw who? Just slow down, I can barely understand you."

"I saw a shadow of the man on my wall at the cabin; he held up a rose and set it down on the stairs. I couldn't breathe. I couldn't even move."

"What happened, did you get hurt?"

"No, nothing happened to me. Once I saw it was the rose that he had in his hand, I ran to the window of the door and tried to look out to see if I could see anything. I couldn't. There was nothing out there but the rose with a note saying that I couldn't hide from him."

"Now I know we'll have to do something. Don't worry about anything Jane, we will take care of everything in the morning. Just come close to me. I'll hold you for the rest of the night. You can tell me everything tomorrow in detail and we will write it down."

I thought Larry has to be the most understanding man, or he is hiding something from me. I really don't think that it is he, but I will always try to keep my eyes open until we figure out who is doing this horrible thing to me. At that very moment Bear comes running up the stairs and jumped on our bed. I just said 'our bed.' I must really love him. I don't know how I could even doubt that he loves me. He is always into everything that I do and involves me in everything that he does.

Our love is and will be impossible to break. He got me a dog, and it has to be the sweetest gift anyone has ever given me. I have always dreamed of the moment that I would find my true love. We would fall in love the first moment we gazed into each other's eyes. It would be hypnotizing and you couldn't turn away. Our love would last forever, kind of like my parents, but without the suicide.

That morning we woke up together and, surprising enough, I wasn't scared anymore. I knew that Larry would be there for me and we will work out everything together. When we sat down for breakfast, I wasn't very hungry. I found myself hating the man that is doing this to me. I didn't even want to know if he left a rose. When Larry went out there he noticed that there was no rose. I thought to myself, 'good.' I really didn't want him to know that I was home yet.

Larry and I had talked things through and I told him everything that had happened. He was a little mad, but nothing happened so it was okay, I guess. We decided to go to the police today and tell them everything. When we got ready, I was shaking. He pulled me aside and said, "Everything will be just fine. I will be there every step of the way. Just stop crying and shaking, I am here for you."

"I know you are, Larry, and you always have been, even though I should have been there for you, as well, and I wasn't."

"Of course you were. Without you I would have been living out on the street."

"What do you mean? Without me you would still be living at home with your son and wife."

He then told me, "Since we are putting everything out in the open, there was another woman before you. Don't worry, I didn't love her and she kept on harassing me."

"So Lynn was telling me the truth when the other girl called."

"Yes. I did have a one-night fling with her, but when you and I got to know each other, there was nothing I could think about besides you. You are the moon and the stars to me and I wanted to tell you because I don't want to lose you because of a lie."

"Oh, how original. I'm the moon and the stars to you. You know what, I will do this by myself. I will go to the police station and do this myself. You mister, just stay here and pack your bags. How could you do this?"

"I wanted to let you know before it was too late. You are very important to me," he said.

"Just remember that while you are packing your bags," I said as I was slamming the door.

While I was driving to the station, I broke down. I really didn't want him to leave. I knew he was sincere to me and he meant it in a good way. I don't know. I just want all of this to end. I started to feel pains in my stomach. I thought to myself, it must be stress, an ulcer or something.

I pulled up to the station and got out. I was frightened to do this all by myself. I didn't know how to begin or even what to say. I sat down on the stairs of the station and began to cry. I was so lost. This guy was stalking me and I feel like he's invading my privacy.

I then got up and started to walk down the stairs and back to my car. I unlocked it and got in. Just as I was shutting the door Larry drove up in a taxi. He threw money at the driver and jumped out. I didn't even try to start my car; it's as if all of my muscles just went limp.

Larry ran up to the car and said that he was very sorry and he will never do anything to hurt me again, but he was not even with me at the time that it happened. It's just he wants to be totally and completely honest with me.

He said, "I have honestly found my true love, even though I am not ready to marry and I am not sure I will be for a long time, it doesn't mean that I will be unfaithful to you."

"I never asked you to marry me in the first place."

"It's just one of those honesty things, again."

I slugged him in the arm after that one and replied, "I love you, too, and I will be happy to spend the rest of my life with you."

"Let's go home and find that warm spot in the bed again. We can come back here tomorrow and talk to them," he proposed.

"I guess so, we can do that."

I then scooted over to the passenger side of the car and Larry got in on the driver's side and we raced home. Once we got back home he walked over to my side of the car and opened the door for me. When we got in the house he handed me a bag of bulbs. I asked him what in the world I was going to do with these.

"I got those for you while you were gone. I thought you were a little sick of roses and I wanted to cheer you up every year."

I looked down at the bag and it was yellow tulips. I looked at him and smiled.

"Thank you so much for thinking of me and I really do love tulips. They come up every year at the same time."

We then walked up the stairs and found our spot on the

bed. He began to rub my back, arms, legs, feet, and neck. I was getting so comfortable that I felt like I was falling into something that I wasn't quite sure of. My body was very relaxed. I felt good and I really didn't want him to stop.

I was thinking to myself, I must be the luckiest damn woman in the world. Either that or my luck is going to run out in a hurry. I then began to think of the future and what things will be like. I thought, what if we have kids and how would this affect his kid.

I knew that it wouldn't really matter. Larry is so level-headed that I know everything will be just fine. Then I started to think of the roses and the tulips and just how wonderful it will be to see them every year and think that Larry got those for me.

Again

Every year in May or so
The flowers bloom
With a tremendous glow

The rain may fall
The water may trickle

But as it stands
With a long stem
And a oval body

The storms come
The wind blows
The stem stays

They may break

With beauty

Bring cheer inside
Standing in the vase
Beauty, pride
Happiness

Every year in May or so
It comes again
It stands again

Rain or shine
It grows

    I felt myself falling asleep while he was rubbing my back so wonderfully. As I slept there, I remember the dream I had very well. I remember it because it scared the living right out of me. I thought I had died and went to hell.
    Well, anyway, as I was sleeping there, I saw a face. It was more like a silhouette on the wall. I was back at the cabin, but Bear wasn't there with me. I was standing in the middle of the room and there was that silhouette. I didn't know what to think; right then I was sitting on a chair at the cabin. I was standing, and then I was sitting.
    His hand was rising up, and at first it looked like the rose in his hand. Then I noticed it was a rose with a dagger at the end of it. As I tried to get out of the chair, all of the sudden my hands and feet were tied with rope. Things keep on appearing in front of my eyes. I couldn't budge an inch; my body was frozen with fear. The door suddenly crept open very slowly.

My hands were sweating and I couldn't breathe any more. I tried to scream out with fear, but nothing came out, not even 'help!' I heard footsteps behind me. I saw nothing walk through that door, nothing. And then there were footsteps, right behind me. They were heavy footsteps. CLUNCK! CLUNCK! I tried to look behind me, but there was nothing.

I looked in front of me and nothing still. Right then a plastic bag went right over my head. I tried to move and see at least who was doing this. His face was distorted, as if there was blood all over it. I couldn't move or breathe. I tried to say 'help.' It didn't even come out that way; I was dying and no one was there to help me.

I heard a noise in the distance. It was Larry. He was saying, 'Wake up! Wake up!' I couldn't move. I didn't know what to do. I felt my head move and the bag become tighter and tighter. It was so hot; I couldn't see.

The guy looked like he even didn't have a face; it was no one in particular. I expect there was blood all over the head, yet I didn't know him or recognize him. Then I felt my body move. He had untied me and was dragging me through the woods by my arms.

I was feeling myself falling in and out of consciousness. Then I felt myself falling and falling and falling and then, splash! I woke up.

Larry had put me in the bathtub and asked me what I was dreaming. He said that my body was very still. He tried waking me, and it didn't work. He didn't know what to do; it was as if I wasn't breathing any more.

I told him about it and he said that he was taking me to the police station, himself, right now. He told me to get dressed and collect my thoughts; we were going, and going now! I got ready and we got in the car. It didn't take very long to get to the station. I knew he was worried about me. I think he thought I had died and came back to life.

When we were in the building I got scared again, but I knew I had Larry there to help me through this. When we walked up to the officer at the front desk, Larry told me to sit down. I overheard him ask the officer, "Is there anyone here we could speak to about someone stalking her?"

The officer said, "There is one person that deals with this, especially, but that person will not be back until tomorrow morning."

Larry asked him, "Is there something we could do now, since we're here?"

"Of course, we have a lot of paperwork that she has to fill out and sign and, then, if she had seen him, we would need a sketch. I would need her to write-in the details: what this person has done along with dates and times. This would be very helpful."

"Thanks, could we take this stuff home and come back tomorrow," Larry asked.

"Yes, of course, you could do that, but be back here in the morning and that officer will be here."

"Thanks, again," Larry said.

He came back and explained everything to me and we went home to write down every detail. We packed up everything we had in a bag so we could bring it to the station tomorrow. I stated each item out loud as Larry typed it on paper. He was so much better at it then I am. Plus, I was still shaking from the dream.

When we got to the police station the next morning we had everything filled out to perfection. I wrote down every little thing I remembered, such as when I thought I saw something outside, every little noise I heard, and the cabin incident. I wrote about the dream which I just had and how it made me feel.

As we sat there waiting for the officer to come in to work we talked about how all of this is affecting me. Larry told me that I had been shaking almost every night while I was sleeping and that he is really starting to worry about me.

I haven't really been working my shifts lately, either. Chris and Sally have been running the business. Larry told me that they had called and asked about me. He told them not to worry about me, and just figure out things amongst themselves. I went in to do the paperwork, but I guess that's about it. I really sat there and thought about it. It really was affecting my life, job, and everyone around me. Right then we were called over to speak to the cop.

He told us that he had looked through everything that we had written.

He said, "I have seen many things in my life about stalkers, but nothing quite like this one."

I asked, "What can we do about it?"

Larry said, "Yes, Jane is really hurting inside more and more everyday. She had that horrible dream yesterday and I thought she had stopped breathing. All of this *has* to stop. You have to do something now about it or else I know this guy is going to hurt her."

I interrupted him, "He knows everything I do; he followed me to the cabin and freaked me out."

The cop told us, "You two have to calm down about this. He hasn't done anything yet and he might be just doing this for fun."

I said, "You don't really have a right to say to us to calm down. You don't know what we have been through with all of this. I haven't been able to work, sleep, or eat. All that is on my mind is this guy and what is he going to do next. I had a dream about him killing me. You have to do more."

Then the cop said, "I will look into this some more, but for now all I can do is have some cops go out to your house and watch it. I will get a team to take turns and make sure that no one tries to do anything funny. I also have to talk to a specialist about all of this and I will call you later this afternoon."

We told him 'thank you' for all of his help and we then went home. I thought to myself this was really getting to me and I really did need to talk to someone about all of this.

Jack said that I had a lot more going on then he would have realized. This rose guy was really freaking me out.

He then suggested hypnotizing me and getting to the bottom of what was really going on.

I asked him, "What do you mean? This whole rose guy was making me insane. That's what probably brought me to this place. I probably went to see a shrink and she dragged me here. That's how I got here."

"Now I know that wasn't it, but I think there is more to it than your not remembering," Jack said.

"I don't understand why you just can't tell me."

"Because this is something you have to deal with yourself. Everyone learns in there own way and this is yours. Go back to your room and write some more."

I really think this whole thing is stupid. As I was walking back to my room, I wanted to remember and forget everything. Just so I can get out of this place. I do remember my stomach hurting more and more.

I decided to go to my doctor and talk to her about why

my stomach was hurting and the other things. Maybe she would have some suggestions about what I could do about all of this. When I called to make the appointment I tried to get in as soon a possible and the quickest was in two weeks. I don't think I would be able to wait that long, but that was the quickest.

Larry told me to try to relax and he would make me something to eat. I told him I really didn't think I could eat anything, but he insisted on me eating something. He is always afraid of me wasting away to nothing. Then I told him I was craving ice cream. He asked me what kind to get and I had told him chocolate-peanut butter is my favorite. But if they didn't have that one, I like chocolate chip cookie dough.

He said he would go and get it, but he didn't want to leave me alone without the cops watching the house. I told him not to worry about it because I am sure that the cops will be here soon. Plus, all we will have to do is double check all the doors and windows and make sure they are locked. I told him in that short of time, I am sure nothing will happen.

He did end up going, but he told me that he would be right back, as soon as possible. I didn't really worry about it, because I knew that he would be back. In horror stories, although, that's when the attackers always come and get the person.

A couple minutes after Larry left the house I heard a loud bang. I went to look to see what it was and it only was the cop slamming his car door. It was so nice for them to show that they were here. At that moment I sat down to watch TV. The news was on and there just had been a murder. It was only a couple blocks away from my house. At that very moment, I ran out to the cop car and asked, "Would that have anything to do with me?"

They replied, "No, we can't really disclose any information on this investigation yet, but I am sure it will have nothing to do with you. Go back in the house now and let us do the work. We will let you know when we find something out on your investigation."

"Thanks, you two, you have been a lot of help."

I turned around and went back into my house. As I was walking back I heard some noises in the bushes and looked over towards them. Right then I took off running into the house, because I was scared out of my wits. I am really starting to hate being scared all of the time.

A little while latter Larry came home and asked me if everything went okay. I told him about the murder a couple blocks away. He told me not to worry, that he was sure that it had nothing to do with the rose man. The cop never called back and I was worrying that something was happening. Larry told me that they were probably caught up with the entire murder situation. I told him that he was probably right.

I totally forgot about the rustling of the bushes. As we were watching TV, I fell asleep and I didn't wake up until the morning. As we were reading the newspaper and drinking our coffee that morning the cop called us back, finally.

He told me that they were no leads on the guy and they figure that nothing will come about it. I was fuming. I didn't even know what to say to him. I handed the phone over to Larry and he talked with him. After he got off the phone with him Larry told me that they would try to continue with the investigation on the rose man, and keep us informed.

They are not going to keep the police watching our house, but they are going to do drive-bys every now and then. I thought that was horrible, they don't even care about me, nor how this is affecting me. I told Larry that I am going to see someone today and talk about everything that is going on. He told me that would probably be a good idea and it might even help me out more on everything.

Chapter Eleven

That same day I went to look for a psychologist to help me. I first started looking in the phone book and I did find someone that would see me that day. About noon I went to the office and it was a woman with whom I had spoken. Her name was Annie, and when we first met she seemed very nice.

I worked with her for about a week straight and I thought I was doing very well. When I went in she said she wanted to do some tests on me. I really didn't know what she had in mind. She told me that they were simple tests and I really didn't need to worry about them.

Just to let you know, I was in the process of selling the business to Sally and Chris. I just couldn't handle it any more; it was getting to be too much for me. They did tell me that they would sell it back to me in a second when I get all of this worked out.

I was still getting roses every three days now, but no notes with them. The pains in my stomach were getting worse, but unfortunately my doctor's appointment wasn't for another week.

I told Annie that I didn't want any tests done, but she informed me that it would be very simple. First I would tell her what I thought when I first looked at some pictures and then she wanted me to try to do something new.

I said okay I will try this picture thing. She told me that it went very well. Then she said that the next one would be for me to write down every dream I had for a week no matter how stupid it might be. I said that should be easy. I made another appointment in a week with her and I felt a little better, but I was still having bad dreams.

A week went by and I wrote down that reoccurring dream I always have along with the one of me going to the bathroom on a toilet in the middle of Target where everyone can see me. Other dreams were of me running as fast as I can in a field with a lot of other people and jumping into the air. Then I began to fly in the sky, until I awoke. Some were of me falling and falling and falling until I awoke from those, too. I wasn't sure what she was going to do with all of these, but I hoped they would help. Today I have my doctor's appointment and I hope she will figure out what is causing my pains.

When I walked in to the room and they told me to put my robe on and wait for the doctor. I began to feel like a lab rat. I know that she will be as nice as possible with me, but my stomach was turning, nonetheless. I was scared. I wanted to know, but then again, I didn't want to know. She walked in and asked me, "So how can I help you today Jane?"

"I have been having problems with my stomach."

"How so?" the doctor asked.

"There have been pains in my stomach, strong and regularly. I have been having a lot of stress lately."

She told me to lie down and she started to press on my stomach. She asked me how long it had been since I had a check-up and I told her a couple of years. I am always healthy so I don't come in every year.

She checked me over and said, "I am not really sure how to tell you this, but let me ask, are you having sex with anyone?"

I told her that I have been with someone for a few months now, but we have been very careful.

She just came out and said it then, "You're pregnant and we need to give you an ultra-sound to figure out how far along you are." She told me to wait a minute and she would be right back with the machine.

I didn't know what to do or say. She probably thought I was crazy because I didn't even say anything. I know my doctor is very professional in everything she does and she is a very good doctor. But I couldn't be pregnant, we were so careful and we used condoms. I have too much going on; I just can't be pregnant right now.

My doctor walked back in and pulled out the jelly that she squirts on my belly. She told me that it probably will be cold to start out, but it will warm up. When she set the monitor on my stomach, I didn't want to look. It was like a little camera that looked right in my belly at every little thing. I ended up looking and a few minutes later we found a heartbeat. She told me that it looks like I am twelve weeks along. No way, I couldn't be. But the ultra-sound machine doesn't lie, she told me.

How am I going to tell Larry? After I found out, I asked her tons of questions and told her about my whole situation. She told me to keep seeing my psychologist. She will probably help me out more now, since I will need it more then ever. She told me not to try to get myself overworked and get lots of rest.

I hopped in my car and started to cry. There's no way Larry will understand any of this and I am already worrying him about all of this too much, anyway. Now I am going to go home and tell him that I am pregnant! I don't know how he is going to take it.

I had to go and see Annie right now. I asked her how am I possibly going to tell him and am I really ready for a child. Annie didn't have any openings that day so I went home. I sat there wondering how I am going to tell him that we are going to have a baby. And it's too late for me to have an abortion, not that I would anyway, but some men aren't really ready for babies. I have heard lots of stories about them telling their girlfriends to get an abortion. I guess it's all up to the person and what their needs are at that time.

When he got home that night, he looked at me and asked me what was wrong. I told him that I really didn't know how to tell him but I had heard some news today and don't know how he was going to take it. "Either you're going to be really happy about it or it is going to make you very mad," I said. "I sat up all night figuring out the best words to describe what is going on and how could I tell you in a calm way.
Larry said, "You know I wouldn't get mad at you."
"I am not quite sure about that, this is really big."
"Nothing is that big that you would think I would get mad at you about it."
"Well in that case read my poem, and tell me what you think of it."
"Okay, then, where is it?" Larry asked.
"I put it on the bed upstairs."
"What in the world is it doing up there."
"I wanted you to be in a different room when you read it."
He started to walk up the stairs and I started to get that puck feeling in my stomach again. I walked over to the couch and went to lie down, as he was reading it.

The poem with only one eye

As your body changes

Your feelings inconsistent

Your dreams are irregular

Something inside

So small
So Delicate

Leaving you with a feeling of exhaustion
Innumerable amounts

Which brings on an inquiry

As your body grows larger

A feeling of injustice

And isolation

Leave you with a feeling of
Inspiration!!!

    I wasn't quite sure what I would do if he didn't like the idea of us being pregnant. I'm not sure if I like the idea of us being pregnant. He was really beginning to take a long time reading it. I started to envision Larry running down the stairs, screaming, "Yes! Yes!" Then I thought that would definitely be a woman's way of doing that. No man would run down the stairs screaming with joy.

No, actually, that man Larry is a calm, cool and collected person. He would walk down the stairs saying, "That's great, baby! How far a long are ya." But I don't know, with everything that's been happening around here and with me, I don't see how this could be good news.

Nothing can ever be perfect for me. Everything is all or nothing. First my parents and then us! There is a little part of me that wants Larry to run down those stairs with excitement, even though I'm not sure I would do the same right now.

I know he loves me and would do anything for me. I will never forget our first kiss in Italy, and how in-control he was. Just then he started to walk down the stairs. I laid there on that couch, in fear of looking up at him. I really did want to, but there was that little part of me that couldn't.

Then his head came around the couch. He wasn't smiling at me; I didn't know what to say at that point. I put my hands over my face and started to cry. He then lifted my feet off the couch to sit down. He grabbed my hands away from my face and said, "That is really great, Jane, and this just might be what you need right now to keep your mind away from the rose man stuff."

"You know we are going to have a baby, don't you?"

"Well, of course I know and I think it's wonderful for us. Now all we have to do is concentrate on all the good this will bring for us."

"You know, I was kind of hoping that you would have run down those stairs with a smile on your face."

"I would have, but I really didn't know how you felt about all of this. I just want to be supportive to you in every way possible," he told me.

"I guess I am glad you're not mad at me!"

"Oh! That's what you were afraid of? Me being mad at you? I wouldn't. You are as precious to me as our baby will be."

I then asked him, "How do you think Lynn will react about all of this?"

"I heard that she was looking for a new guy in her life, already. I wouldn't be hurt if she did find out about this, but I am sure she won't. I am sure she won't find anyone to date her, because no one will be able to put up with her crap."

"Well, I haven't heard you talk about her that way in a long time."

He then said, "I won't talk about her again. Come here, I want to give you a great, big hug."

I then said to him, "No matter what, we will work this out right? I really want us to be happy. That's all I have ever wished for."

Only Wish

I wish
I wish
For unconditional love
As tornadoes are to wind
And hurricanes are to rain

I wish so hard
I wish so long
To find the one
With no etching on his bark
Or fallen leaves

I wish with my heart
I wish with my soul
To see my shooting star
Falling with me on my left

As I blow my dreams away
And wait for my fantasy
Hoping that someday
He will be here to stay!

"I also want you to know, you are that fantasy of mine. You are my dreams and my future," I told him.

He looked at me and said with a smile on his face, "You know I love you, just as much as you love me. I may not be as great with the words as you are, but I do love you. And it is very important for you to know I am here for you."

"Thank you, Larry, I always love hearing that from you."

"What are you going to do about your psychologist? Will you still be going to her?" Larry asked with wonder.

"Of course. I told my doctor everything and she suggested to me that I continue with Annie and get lots of rest."

He started to get that sexy smile on his face again. I definitely know now that he is happy about all of this. That night when we went to sleep, he had held my stomach all night long.

He then whispered in my ear, "I hope we have a girl."

Chapter Twelve

When I started to look back on the life I had, I knew that it hasn't been very fair to me. I knew that I was pregnant at one time, and either I lost the baby or someone is taking care of it for me. I was really thinking of getting hypnotized by Jack, but I wasn't sure if I should or not. I just want this whole thing over.

I saw that favorite weeping willow of mine and I was wondering what it would be like to be that tree. To have no feelings, just to sit there and just be alive. Not to worry about anything in life. It sounded so relaxing to me. There was the smallest part of me that would like to be that tree.

That afternoon when I went to see Jack I finally told him that I would agree to him hypnotizing me today. I told him that it is absolutely driving me crazy not knowing what happened to me.

He then told me, "It will only work if you put every ounce of what you have into it. You need to relax and calm yourself as much as possible, just so you will be able to dig deep and tell me everything."

I said, "That sounded fair enough, so where do we start."

He told me to get comfortable and lie down on the couch and listen to him. All I remember is Jack telling me to relax and to think of a peaceful place to be. When I awoke, I knew nothing.

I asked him, "So what happened? What did I say to you? Did I mention anything about the baby?"

Jack told me to try to remember what I had told him. I can't believe he had the guts to say that to me. I told him if that is what your answer was going to be I would have never agreed to do anything of the sort.

"I want answers and I want them now!"

I then stood up and started yelling at him with so much anger built up. I told him I wanted him dead and it just wasn't fair to me. He has been torturing me since I walked in this place a little over two years ago. Now, he should be the one that is to be tortured.

I then picked up his coffee cup full of coffee and threw it against the wall as hard as I could. I was screaming at him with a lot of anger. It was as if it had been building up inside of me and I had reached that point.

I was screaming over and over, "I will get you back. I will get you back for everything." It was as if someone else had spoken those words—or was it. I was screaming. "You have caused so much pain inside, pain that will never go away." I was telling him that he was the one, he was the one that should be in my place.

During that whole time of me yelling at him, he didn't flinch or even show any sign of an expression. He just kept on telling me that I should sit down and think of what I was saying to him. I just couldn't relax. I had finally agreed to do this and he betrayed me.

It wasn't fair to me, or anyone else that has been in my life. Right at that moment a security guard came in and shot something into my arm. I began to feel a lot more relaxed—I was stuck. It was as if I couldn't breathe or even move. I was frozen inside, everything was becoming blurry. Then I heard voices in the background.

Jack told the guy, "Just leave her on the couch, I will take care of her. Our session is not over yet, we still have a lot to talk about."

I asked, "So, what are your plans for me?"

He said, "I have been waiting for this moment for

many years now."

"What are you talking about," I asked him while my words were beginning to slur.

"What am I talking about? You are the one that should know, you have known this whole time. Pretending that you don't, you're just afraid of what's out there."

So I asked him, "So what's out there, what's the mystery?"

"Nothing, you have nothing, your life is a lie. No business, no parents, no Larry and most of all—no baby."

"What are you talking about? What's a lie?"

I was starting to fall asleep. Right then I felt a slap on my face. I opened my eyes, I could barley feel that.

He told me to, "Stay awake. I am not finished with you. What do you really think happened to you in your so-called fantasy life."

"I don't know what you're talking about, so why don't you share your news with me."

Jack had an expression on his face that was starting to scare me. He just kept pacing back and fourth right in front of me. His head was down and his forehead was wrinkled. I didn't know what to say. I felt my body floating away from me.

Before I knew it, I was waking up in my room. The sun was shining; it just looked like a beautiful day out there. I walked over to look out my door window and right then I noticed that my door was locked. My door is never locked, maybe at first, but not lately. I walked back over to my bed and sat down.

I wanted answers so badly I couldn't stand it any longer. Jack went all crazy on me. I just kept on thinking of what he told me. All I have to do is think back, and just try to remember. Every time I think about it, nothing happens. I think of what I had written and now I really wonder if it was real.

Jack told me that I had nothing left. I must have something left or was my life a lie to me. Is nothing truly real or does our perception of what is supposed to be real, deceiving our reality of life? You look to someone for answers and all they have to tell you is 'to just think harder. All you have to do is remember.' Just remember, that is a load of crap to me.

Something just flew away
I tried to grab it
It was just beyond my reach
A little part of me
Just began to flee
I felt empty
Something disappeared
A great part of me!

Just then my door opened and Jack walked through it. I turned my head; I wanted nothing to do with him.

I told him, "Get out, I don't want you in my room. I don't even want to see your face. Why didn't you just kill me when you had the chance."

"You do remember, after all!"

"So, it is true. At first I wasn't sure. But now it all makes perfect sense, you're that rose guy," I said to him.

"What? How could I have been him? No, I'm the man with the dog."

"What, I am so confused. So, why would you have agreed to kill me? I just don't understand any of this."

"To tell you the truth, I was hired by Annie to watch you. She had explained everything that was going on in your life since the police found nothing. She was very concerned about your welfare. She gave me a call right after she found out that you were pregnant. We had been bumping into each other here and there. So it was very easy for me to ask you out.

Believe it or not we walked our dogs together many times. You began to open up to me and tell me everything about your life. About you're unfortunate situations with Larry and his ex. About the rose guy and everything that he was doing to you and about you being pregnant."

"I would have never betrayed Larry in such a way. He loved me and took care of me," I told him.

"Yes I know, but he began to go on more than one business trip a month. You began to become very disturbed about the whole thing and were starting to feel alone and empty inside."

I told him, "I don't really remember any of that. Hold on a minute, why did you yell at me yesterday and say all of those things to me."

He said to me, "Sometimes anger gets everything out in the open. It makes people realize more then they want to know."

I asked him, "So why would you have killed me? Why did you ever agree to that?"

"I didn't. We were walking our dogs one day and you began to feel a lot of pain. You suddenly let go of the leash and fell to the ground. Well to make a long story short, I ended up bringing you to the hospital and you lost your baby. I thought maybe you were blaming me for that."

"Maybe I did, I don't recall any of that. So did anyone ever find anything out about the rose guy?"

"No, no one did, but one night I started to follow Larry around. I followed him on one of his business trips. All of those were a scam to get to other women. He thrived on other women; he ended up bringing them on trips and seduces them in a way that seemed so sincere. It made all of the women feel loved and not alone any more."

"How do you know any of this? How do you know how those women possibly felt? All of this is a lie; I just can't believe any of it."

Jack told me, "You know how you opened up when you began to know me. Well I made friends with all of those women and they began to tell me things."

"And what about the rose guy, what did you find about him?"

"My theory is that he is Larry, possibly," Jack told me with certainty.

"I can't believe any of this. Get out; just get out of my room right now. It just can't be possible. There is no way under any circumstances that Larry is the rose man. He was just so loving and kind. Get out of here," I was telling him as I was pushing him out of my room.

"I will be back in a few hours. Just try to think about what I have told you," he was saying to me as I was furiously shutting the door in his face.

I can't remember any of the things that he told me. We never did talk about why I came here, what happened to my dog, or why Jack cared so much about me. He didn't even know me until we had started talking.

Larry was the one that was always for me. He even told me not to worry about the rose guy. "He hasn't done anything yet to you and he probably won't." It was as if he was never concerned about it until it got serious.

Maybe I gave him too much freedom. Maybe I was wrapped up in my life too much and that is why he was screwing around with other women. What am I talking about? Larry never had sex with other women. I just can't believe that he would mess around behind my back. I ended up falling asleep while I was thinking about all of this.

When I awoke Jack was sitting in a chair next to my bed. He had startled me.

I asked him, "What about my dog and my house? Whatever became of them and why am I here? You're hiding something from me and I want to know everything."

Jack ended up telling me everything. At first I couldn't believe him or maybe I didn't want to. Something inside of me blocked out everything. That is why I couldn't remember any of it until I started writing it down on paper. Even though I never solved why I was here and how I came here, I did find out a lot about myself. It's just this awful thing happened to me.

Jack told me when I lost my baby I started to repress everything. I began to push Larry away more and more. My nightmares began to get a lot more serious. I didn't work; I stopped taking Bear for walks. I sat on the couch, comatose, with the TV. I didn't talk to anyone; I wouldn't even go outside anymore.

Finally Larry brought me to the hospital and left me on the front steps. When Jack told me all of this I couldn't believe any of it, it made no sense to me. Why am I okay now?

I asked Jack if I could call someone that I knew. He asked me if I really thought that was a good idea. Do I really want to bring all of those insane past memories back to me?

Chapter Thirteen

I sat in my room for weeks and weeks, thinking about all that had happened. All I really could think about now is getting out. Just to be out of this place is what I want right now. I started to go more and more places around the building. I acted as if I didn't care about my past.

Jack and I grew to become great friends. We talked about the future and what was ahead for us. I told him I wanted to get out and explore the world that was ahead of me. There is so much out there that I am missing.

He had asked me if I am really ready and, of course, I am. What could be better then exploring every aspect of life? I told him I am ready for everything right now; just give me my next step.

That very day he ended up signing my papers and I moved in with him. I had nothing, but Jack was very kind to me. He bought me everything—clothes, CD's and, of course, he had my dog. I asked him how he ended up with Bear and he said that Larry had moved and didn't want it anymore. He put it in the paper as 'a great dog looking for a new home.' Jack called him and Larry just gave it to him and has been taking care of the dog this whole time. I ended up thanking him and gave him a great big hug.

That next day Jack ended up going to work and had explained to me that dwelling on the past is wrong and I should look to the future for answers. Also, he said if I needed anything, that I was to call him right away and he would figure out a way to get it for me. He didn't want me to go anywhere without asking him first. This is my first step to recovery and I should stay around the house today.

Tomorrow he had off so he was going to bring me around and show me the town.

I couldn't wait; I have been giving him this show. I really want to figure out why I was there and I wanted the truth. I grabbed the phone book and tried to look up Larry. I couldn't find him anywhere, so I tried to look up Chris and Sally. They weren't in there either. I was beginning to think that I was in a different town. My business wasn't in the book and Larry's restaurant wasn't even in there. So I called a taxi and asked him to pick me up and drive me to the library.

When I got there I asked librarian to show me to the phonebooks from the past years. I started looking through them and I still found nothing. I then asked the librarian to help me and she had never heard of any such places. I left the library and felt even more lost. I must have been in a different town. That's the explanation to Jack not wanting me to go anywhere.

When the taxi driver picked me back up, I had asked him about the places and he knew nothing. When I got home, I dialed 411 for information and they couldn't even find those places anywhere.

I didn't know what to think; maybe they closed and it isn't in their computer anymore. That has to be it—that was the best explanation. I still couldn't let Jack know what I had done. So I started to write a poem to let him know that I was home and working on it.

Dreams

What a wonderful place
So sweet

Not even touching reality
To feet

Wind through the hair
So bright

Feeling the warmth
A silver light

A touch of love
The tears

To break the flight
Have fears

To have the colors
They lack

Of an iridescent glow
Now so black

When Jack got home he asked me what I had done all day. I told him I just sat around and wrote a poem, played with Bear and watched TV.

"Oh, so you didn't explore the world today?"

"What do you mean, I was here all day."

"Well you think you have me fooled, I know what you were doing. You're just a mere lab experiment to me,"

Jack said.

"I'm not quite sure what you're getting at, what experiment.?"

"Oh, you think I am so benign to everything you have done, I am just merely holding myself back. I have held an experiment over your life."

"For how long? And for what kind of experiment?" I asked him.

Then Jack went on to say, "It all started back in September of 1998. There was a group of us trying to figure out the best experiment of all. We came up with this one: we wanted a girl that had strong feelings about herself. One that could put up a fight, and who lasts more than five minutes. One that was troubled and had nothing, more or less—a street girl. Especially not one from around here though. We needed someone that no one would miss. We started looking on the Internet under the police files."

I interrupted him by asking, "So am I a runaway? Without a family? Please, this would be the time to tell me the truth. I desperately need the answers right now. I feel my life depends on it. So is nothing true that I know of my life?"

Jack then told me, "Well, something has to be true, because I don't remember feeding you all of that information. But, pretty much all of the things that you had written down was not true."

"So, all of my feelings, everything that I thought, was untrue? Even my parents are dead, or are they?"

"Well to get back to what I was telling you, we had gone through all of the reports of petty crimes. We looked through all of everyone's credentials. It took us months to find the right person," Jack told me.

"So I was a problem-child. What did I do in my previous life?"

"You used to work in retail sales, until they found you stealing clothes. Your parents ended up kicking you out of their house. They weren't your real parents, anyway. The way it sounded, you were a problem-child to start out with and we ended up hunting you down."

"Are you guys insane? So you have all worked on this for over three years now. How did you do it and without anyone knowing? You mean no one once asked for me?"

"By the way, my real name is Lane and your name is Jade. I thought it would be a name that would coincide with each other. It would make us one. I put my thoughts and feelings in your brain while hypnotizing you.

You were really easy to do. I saw you walking on the street, walked right up to you and asked you if you wanted to make some money. You told me that you're no hooker and were insulted by me. I introduced myself as 'Jack' and said to you that you could get hypnotized for free and get anything you wanted by agreeing to this experiment that I was doing."

"So, I agreed to do this right away?"

"No, not at first, but I had given you my card for later. A couple of days had gone by and you gave me a call. You asked me all about it."

"So, you lied to me?"

"Not exactly, I just didn't tell you the whole truth."

"So, you basically kidnapped me?" I said.

"I just wanted to do this one thing and write a book about it. You basically started that one for me, too."

"Well, isn't that convenient for you. You take my life away from me and now you're telling me about it. You know what, I would like to go. I want to go and live my life now."

"You don't want my help in any way–money, clothes, anything that could get you started?"

"No, just a ride to town."

I was very surprised, but Lane did give me a ride that day. I see no visible abuse done to me. I felt good all around. He dropped me off without saying anything but slipping me an envelope when I left the car.

I was finally out of there, I had my life back and now I have to find my parents and who I really am. I ended up standing outside a coffee shop, while he drove off in his car. I looked down and opened up the white envelope and there was his card and money. Oh, about a couple hundred dollars.

I was feeling hungry, so I walked in and got a café mocha and a bagel with cream cheese and strawberry jam on it, too. I then decided to go to the police station and just see if they knew who I was. Also to see if they could find out where I am from.

I walked up and asked them, "Can you please help me find out who I am? I have amnesia and I would like to find my home."

They ended up calling someone to help me out. They took my blood, fingerprints, and ended up asking me tons of questions. I waited there for a while in the chairs, not knowing if they were going to find out anything about my life. I then went to get something to drink and when I got back, I sat down.

Finally a guy walked out and asked me if my name was Jade. I told him I wasn't sure, but the police were checking it out for me. "Well, I was just called in here, because I am your husband," he said.

When do you know when?

It's time to close your eyes

As the time awaits

To make our lives

Fulfilled to the fullest

To make our dreams

Become extraordinary

We understand

Why we are here, and what

Needs to be done